KSENIA

AND THE WORLD OF INSPIRATION

THE SERIES OF THE BIRD WITH BLUE BLOOD

KSENIA

AND THE WORLD OF INSPIRATION

BOOK ONE

MOE. S.D

Library of Congress Control Number:		2019906988
ISBN:	Hardcover	978-1-7960-3915-3
	Softcover	978-1-7960-3914-6
	eBook	978-1-7960-3913-9

Print information available on the last page.

Rev. date: 06/10/2019

To order additional copies of this book, contact:
Xlibris
1-888-795-4274
www.Xlibris.com
Orders@Xlibris.com
795634

CONTENTS

ABOUT THE AUTHOR

Moe is a professional painter of contemporary art who has presented his art everywhere in the world from Dubai to New York, Illinois, and Houston.

A painter from childhood, he attended Fine Art school, gaining a Bachelor's degree, followed by a Master's degree from Eastern Illinois University. His oil paintings were first showcased in an exhibition titled "The Bid of Spring" in Dubai, which displayed more than 24 of his works.

Moe's paintings uniquely portray his life stories and his life's devotion to following his inspiration. His artwork is based on three principal elements; the inspiration, the story behind the inspiration, and the painting itself.

Of his work, Moe says, "I believe there are two types of inspiration; object and nonobject. Inspirations that are objects are those in the real world that we can see and touch, but they are limited, and can only be interacted with using our physical senses; for example, trees, animals, and the body are all object inspirations.

"On the other hand, nonobject inspiration cannot be seen in the real world, but is limitless; no space or time can confine it.

"After the inspiration comes the story, which is shown to an artist in the World of Inspiration, and must then be brought into the real world using tangible colours, shapes, and real-world tools like paint and canvas."

INTRODUCTION

The Author's Inspiration

"My Dream and the Real Story of the Bird with Blue Blood - The inspiration for My Writing and Painting"

One night several years ago, I had a beautiful dream. In my dream, I saw myself as a bird, looking at an abstract, shaded spectrum with a beautiful shape inside it. A beautiful voice came from the colors, its cadence like notes of music tinkling in my ears.

"Do you know me? Do you know what color you are?" the voice asked.

I did not recognize the shape, because the light surrounding it was very bright, but the voice has stayed in my mind ever since.

"No," I said, "but you are the most beautiful thing I have ever seen."

The voice said, "I am waiting for you, do not be late."

"But how will I know I am talking to you?" I replied.

"You will know it's me; I will tell you that I like the color blue."

"I will find you, I promise. I will never give up!" I shouted.

I woke up suddenly, my body filled with energy. "She is waiting for me!" I shouted, "She is going to tell me that she likes blue. I must find her!"

The next few months passed slowly, one after the other. Each morning gave me fresh hope that I would finally find her, but each night I did not only brought disappointment.

Her words repeated in my mind. *"I will tell you I like the color blue. Do not be late."*

I shared my dream with my family and best friend. They mocked me, saying that I was insane to believe in a dream. But I knew it was real; a vision. I felt it in my bones.

As the days went by, I started to lose my patience and decided that I must do something. I wanted to find a way to communicate with people through my art, in the hope that it might help me find her.

I created seven paintings, each one an abstract portrait of a girl holding a flower. In each, the flower was a different color, and only one held the blue tones I longed for a girl to say she liked. I hid the painting with the blue flower among the others, and photographed them to carry with me as I searched desperately to find the girl who would tell me she liked the color blue.

I started by showing those pictures to everyone who I met, never telling them what I hoped to hear. I showed my pictures to many different people—relatives, friends, and strangers I saw wherever I went. I asked the flight attendant on one of my journeys if she liked paintings, and when she said yes, I showed her the photos. In response, she said, "I like them," but she did not say, "I like the color blue."

The hope in my heart never died, but every day I did not hear those words became more difficult. One day, everything changed.

At Lakeland College, in one of my English classes, I met my fate, and she made me feel a way I have never felt before, filling my heart with peace.

A girl named cheyanne was one of my classmates. She seemed nice, but I was scared to even look at her. Every day, I planned to talk to her, but I always backed out; more shy and scared than I had ever been before. I wanted to ask her if she liked blue, but whenever I got close to her, I would lose my courage. My eyes avoided her whenever she looked at me, but when she looked away, I couldn't take my eyes off of her.

One time, I busied myself by pretending to read some blank paper in front of me, but I glanced at her and saw her smiling at me.

I gathered myself, and asked her, "Do you like paintings?"

After a moment of silence, she replied, "I like the color blue."

The world froze in front of me. I opened my eyes wide, choking with excitement. Had she really said she liked blue, even before I had showed her the picture?

I kept looking into her eyes. When uncontrollable tears touched the white sheets of paper on my desk, I finally broke the silence. "You are the one!" I shouted. "I have been looking for you for a long time, and I have found you at last. You are the dream that has been growing in my soul."

All my classmates and my English teacher just stared.

Embarrassed, I left the class, but I was as happy as if I was a bird flying high in the sky.

The next time I saw her, I gave her a painting, *"A Flower in the Beautiful Shade of Blue."*

"cheyanne," I said, handing it to her, "this is for you."

Our whole class stared, confused.

"Did you draw this?" she asked.

"Yes, because you said that you like blue."

Our classmates gathered around her, curious to see the painting.

I was happy, but another strange feeling rose in my heart, filling the world around me with darkness and fear. I left the class to sit in the lobby.

Soon, cheyanne followed me, coming to sit beside me. I told her about my dream and all the difficulties I had had in my journey to find her. I told her that she was the reason for my existence, and that I had been painting her every day but destroying the paintings after I finished them as I felt she was from a different world. I told her I had kept my promise and looked for her.

Sudden warm tears fell on my hand, and I remembered my dream and what the voice had said: *"I am waiting for you. Do not be late."*

Just then, I heard someone calling her. It was a man.

She leaned over the table and said sadly, "You came late." Without another word, she got up and left, but her eyes locked with mine, saying, *"I love you. I want to go with you."*

"She has a boyfriend, and you came late," a voice in my head said out of nowhere. "Look, she is with another man, sailing in his boat. You should leave your journey here."

"If she is on a boat with another man, I wish to be like a bird flying near it, nothing more," I replied.

However, because she had been my dream for so long, I could not bear to see her with another man. The pain was like thousands of arrows piercing my whole body, and I was like a bird falling from the sky into the deep dark ocean to rest on its sandy bed. I felt as if my blood and feathers were everywhere around me. I decided to draw my story using my feather as a brush and my blood as paint. I did a painting for every year of her age, and shades of blue shone in all of them.

"In my vision as a bird, my blood is blue. All of me is," I murmured to myself one day. I realized that my vision had said she would tell me she loved the colour blue because I was blue, and she loved me.

She saw my true form, a bird with blue blood who is inspired by the World of Inspiration.

cheyanne was my dream, and I hoped to meet her for a long time, but all too quickly she became a dream again. I have no hope to find her again; she has gone forever with another man, but she still inspires me.

My dream represents my inspiration from another world, but it is cheyanne who is my inspiration in the real world. The moment we met, my dream became reality, and my two inspirations collided to determine the shape, colors, subject, and style of my work. As a result, cheyanne is going to be the subject of my new exhibition, as well as having been my inspiration.

The first part of my paintings exhibited will be abstract—as she was to me before I found her—then they will begin to reflect reality—as she became real in my life—and will finally be abstract again—as she has once again become a dream, and will be so forever.

The last painting will have a feather and a blue flower on her dress. It will be to show my gratitude, because she inspires me, and will for the rest of my life.

CHAPTER ONE

Beginnings

It had been a beautiful house at the top of the hill, set just two miles away from the city of Alyssum and made of beautiful red brick. The house had been built on the west side of the ocean, where the water's color perfectly complimented the colors of the sky. The view it gave of the sea, the ebb and flow of the blanket of blue spreading over the earth, was spectacular. From the house, the horizon was no more than a thread separating the beauty of the dark blue ocean from the light blue of the sky. The big windows of the house were one of its best features, allowing nature to surround the occupant. They were like a giant canvas, and the surrounding landscape was all at once the artist, the subject, and the color palette.

The sunrises and sunsets that illuminated it best had once bestowed a glorious vista upon all the people of the city of Alyssum. They had viewed the house as one of the most inspiring places on earth, and spent many happy hours simply gazing at it while camping in the forest to its north. To the west of the house lay an idyllic beach, where the sand stretched like a white, powdery carpet along the shore to the water's edge, covered by drops of seawater as it ebbed away from the coast. From above, they took on the appearance of pearls or mirror shards reflecting the sunlight, and shone like silver dust on the surface of the crags near the shore.

Now, though, the beauty and inspiration that had once attached itself to the house were long gone. It was still unique, and continued to dominate the landscape, but its attractiveness had been replaced by a sense of its true evil and sadness. Fear, not wonder, now enveloped the city as its population looked upon the house that loomed overhead, and people who had once dreamed of living in it now never dared to even venture in its shadow.

*   *   *

This story began when a rich and famous physician by the name of Balthazar decided to build a house about two miles out of the city on the top of the hill. Balthazar was one of the best doctors in the city of Alyssum, and well known among the people by his love of—and support for—all kinds of art.

Since he was a child, he had wanted to be an artist, but just as his dad had requested before he died, Balthazar had become a doctor instead. His love of art had never left him, though, and he had dreamed of having a home artists could freely use as a studio to practice their craft away from all the stifling rules and regulations imposed by the Nature School of Art, the leading art school in the city.

He had always rejected the idea that art could be controlled, and was famous for once having said, "Rules limit the talent of artists, imprisoning them in a confined place where there is no space for their creativity to grow and for new ideas to be brought to life."

And so it was that Dr. Balthazar made his house into a remarkable place where artists could escape just that. One of the main features of the house was the main hall, which he designed as a gallery to hold musical concerts and exhibit all kinds of art in. Many famous artists and architects participated in the designing and furnishing of the house, and thus it was a work of art in itself. Sculptures and murals were everywhere to be found—both inside and in the grounds—to inspire artists that worked within it.

Being such a freely creative space, It was inevitable that the artists who worked within it would generate new kinds of art, and therefore just as inevitable that it would bring Balthazar face to face with the tradition of the Nature School of Art, which began to see him as an opponent. However, he persisted with his message of unrestrained creativity, and day by day he established respect for his new ideas, which a vast proportion of both artists and Alyssum's people quickly became attracted to. The musical shows that took place in spring, summer, and autumn brought growing crowds up the hill to attend all the house events.

Dr. Balthazar lived happily in the house with his beautiful wife and his newborn child, but not for very long. Two years after moving in, everything turned dark, and the picture of beauty, peace, and harmony that the house had been left the world to be replaced by another, darker picture, one that told sad and strange stories about the house. A tragedy occurred. Dr. Balthazar disappeared, and his wife and child were found unconscious at the bottom of the hill halfway between their home and the city. It was a shock—a big shock—to all who knew them.

Balthazar's wife could not say much about the incident, as she lost her memory and was hospitalized for several months afterward. All she remembered was knowing that an unseen evil existed in a secret room in her house. Six months after Balthazar, she and her child also disappeared, and in the many years that followed, no one saw or heard anything about them again.

At first, some people accused the Nature School of Art of killing Dr. Balthazar and his family so they could stop his project of abolishing their rules for art, but they soon realized there was a real evil in existence. Two of Balthazar's wife's rescuers—servants who had been on their way to the house in the early morning—told of an evil tree with multiple faces moving down the hill, drawing closer to Balthazar's wife and her child. Many stories about the incident followed. One told of a stranger who came from the other side of the sea and cast a curse to bring sorrow and pain to the Balthazar family. This story was supported by the Nature School of Art, which warned the curse was punishment for Balthazar's attempts to change the rules and spirit of art.

As the stories of artists and famous actors going up the hill and disappearing grew, so too did the fear in Alyssum's people, and they soon stopped going up the hill themselves. They had never seen the evil stranger who placed the curse, but believed he had come from a land far away, somewhere on the other side of the ocean. Some people believed he stayed in the house, waiting for a new victim, but others said he visited the house for a few days once a year, announced by the red candlelight that shone from the abandoned house for several days in the winter. It seemed intent to reach all the homes in the city, and when it burned, its reflection could be seen in every window-pane in the city below.

Some took it as a sign that stranger had arrived in the city, seeking a victim to steal the soul of before he went back over the sea again. Their fear was enormous, and made people weave even stranger stories about the evil in the house. No one dared to be close to the edge of 'The Hill'—as it was known—during winter, but in spring, summer, and autumn, most people still felt brave enough to camp near the hill and enjoy the beautiful nature and outstanding views.

Even then, they would not venture too close to the fence around the house. It was as if beauty lay on one side, and fear and death lay on the other. This made the area all the more curious, and on any given day, people could be found standing as close to the fence as they dared; looking at the house and wishing they knew more about it.

*   *   *

Richard Ellison was one of many artists amazed by the stories that he heard about both the beauty of the house and its terrors, and resolved that one day he would go and discover the truth about it. Richard was a young artist, aged just 21, who had moved with his mother Lauren to the city two years before to pursue his dream. Naturally, he had joined the Nature School of Art, as it was widely considered to be one of the most renowned schools in the world.

Richard grew up in the city of Springfield, about 50 miles away from Alyssum. He had loved painting nature since he was a child, and had worked very hard to develop his skills as a landscape painter. Since they had moved to the city of Alyssum, Richard and his mother had rented a small house in the suburbs, about ten miles away from the center.

As was its practice, the Nature School of Art had organised an outdoor trip for its students to give them an opportunity to be in touch with nature, use different kinds of subjects, and enhance their ability to draw outside of traditional studios. Richard was excited at the news—he had never been on such a trip before, and even better, as fate would have it, they would be visiting a spot near 'The Hill.'

CHAPTER TWO

Meeting Davenport

Although Richard had a perfectly valid reason for making a trip to the area—to use the nature there as a subject for his sketching—he did not want to tell his mother about his plan, for he knew that she would never let him go if she knew the truth. Instead, all he said to her was that he was going on a school trip to do live painting as part of his program, carefully neglecting to tell her where. He was excited to take the trip, and could not wait to see the house he had heard so many stories about.

* * *

As soon as the bus arrived at their destination, one of the two teachers supervising the trip instructed them to choose a spot and start painting there, but warned them not to cross the fence atop the hill. Fortunately for them, most of the students seemed so eager to be out of the studio that all that was on their minds was to choose a spot and draw.

Richard was amazed by the beauty of the hill, and took a long look at the Balthazar house, which sat some distance up it. He did many sketches of the house from different angles, before deciding to continue wandering around.

The beauty of the area fascinated him. He walked on between the trees on the hillside until he saw a man—who looked to be in his sixties—sitting on a tall tree, head bowed.

There was a warning sign affixed to it; "*If you love life, do not deceive by snakeskin. Its sharp teeth will fill your blood with poison.*"

"What strange words!" Richard murmured as he read.

The man lifted his head up and met Richard's gaze with a mocking smile. "Go away, young man, or it will bite you."

"Who on earth wrote those foolish words? I do not see any reason to hang such a sign on this beautiful tree! It's just spreading fear and telling lies."

"You're an outsider, aren't you? *I* wrote this sign a long time ago, two years after the Balthazar incident."

"I'm not from here. I grew up in the city of Springfield, and moved here with my mother to study. What on earth made you do that?" Richard asked.

"My job," the man replied simply, and with that he moved the metal sign further up the tree without any effort, even though it looked too heavy for a man his age to lift. "Richard, can you help me fix the board?"

"How do you know my name?" Richard replied incredulously

In answer, the man just smiled and said, "Come up, Richard, and help me."

"No, I won't do that. I will not be part of deceiving others."

"Then go, son. Do not waste my time, or yours. Leave me to do my job."

"Why do some call it the House of Agony?" Richard asked, pointing toward the house up the hill.

The man was silent, ignoring him.

"OK. If I help you, will you tell me the real story? I have heard so many of them, and I want to know the truth about the house," Richard relented.

The man smiled again. "Yes, I will tell you the whole story."

With that, Richard climbed the tree to help him, and both fixed the sign. When it was done, the man stopped for a moment. "Have you heard the legendary story of the bird of agony?"

"Never. What happened?"

"Once a year, it flew over the sea to where a small city lay amid the mountains. It flew all over the city until it chose a house, then stayed in that house for three days, singing a song of death to bring bad luck and sorrow to those that lived there. It was said that no one ever saw the bird of agony itself, only its shadow on the walls of the chosen house. Its song was only heard in the head of the one it chose. No matter what the victim did, and no matter where they went, it was said that the song would not stop until it had taken their soul. It's said that the victim's screaming could be heard all over the city, but no one could ever help them. After it was done, the bird flew home, taking with it the soul of whoever was chosen."

Richard was completely confused after hearing this story, but the man had not yet finished.

"This story left a strong impression on the way that the people of Alyssum think. Since the incident happened to Balthazar's family, the lights of one of the rooms of the house have been seen to burn red during winter, and for three days the candlelight acts like a call reaching each house. It can be seen from everywhere in the city, even on foggy nights. Everyone becomes scared on the nights when the weather changes suddenly, the world becomes blue, and the wind blows the quietness away with its terrible momentum. Fear is the only thing the people know then."

"I heard about the red light, but I haven't seen it yet; I went back to Springfield to visit some friends last winter. Is it true?"

"Yes, and you will see it this winter if you stay. It will reach everyone in the city, attempting to absorb the life, joy, and happiness from Alyssum and turn it to emptiness."

"That's why you built the fence and are putting up all these signs?"

"It's not just me, the people of the city also built a wood fence adorned with signs at the north border. They are there to warn everyone, to keep them away from the hill and ensure they never cross the land to the house. Come with me. I want to show you something before I go."

Both took a walk along the fence until the man stopped abruptly at another large sign.

"Look at that one," the man said, pointing. "Read it, Richard."

"'You may have the choice to go there or not, but remember it will be the most dangerous adventure you have ever had in your life'", Richard read aloud. He was suddenly curious to know exactly who he was talking to. "You know my name, but can I ask yours?"

"My name is Steve Davenport." The man continued walking along the fence, as though he was leading Richard to a specific destination.

Richard continued walking, failing to notice the long distance that now separated him from his classmates. They kept walking until Richard saw an old house by the edge of the fence.

"There's my place," announced the man.

"Where? That old house?"

"No, behind that big tree."

"If this is not your house, then why did you bring me here?"

"Once it was my house, Richard, but not anymore. I am about to leave, but I have a request for you. I wonder if you can help?"

"Yes, sir. I'd be happy to help you if I can." Richard felt very connected with Mr. Davenport somehow, almost as though he had known him for years.

"I want you to draw many pictures of this house and give them to Lauren."

"Lauren? Who is she? Do I know her?"

Suddenly, many birds flew out of the big tree, distracting Richard. As he turned to watch the birds fly over the house, the old man said, "Your mother, Richard."

"M-My mother? Do you know my mother?" Richard stuttered in shock.

When he turned around to face Mr. Davenport, there was no sign of him. Richard called his name many times, but there was no response. Richard felt scared, his mind whirling with questions.

Why did he bring me here? And why did he want me to show pictures of this house to my mother? What does all of that mean?

He looked again at the old house standing by itself. It may have been old, but was still beautiful, surrounded by a large field filled with flowers of all kinds.

Richard found himself stood between two houses—one big and on the hill and the other old and small on the edge of the hill. They were facing each other, both hiding their secrets. They shared a truth that had been hidden from the world. He quickly started to sketch as many pictures of the old house as he could until the sun was about to set. As soon as he finished, he ran for more than twenty minutes, until he reached the school bus. The other students were waiting in line ready to get on board, entirely oblivious to Richard's cryptic encounter with the strange old man.

CHAPTER THREE

Lauren's Secret

It was late evening, and the sky had grown dark. Lauren was in the kitchen packing up some freshly-baked cookies, preparing the dinner and waiting for Richard to arrive home when she heard footsteps coming from the living room. "Richard? Is that you?"

"Yes, Mom, I'm home."

"How was your trip?"

"It was great!" Richard walked into the kitchen and kissed his mother.

She wrinkled her nose in feigned disgust. "I know you probably have a lot to tell me, but go change your clothes and take a shower while I finish getting dinner ready."

"OK, Mom."

*   *   *

Richard went up to his room and sat heavily on his bed, thinking about his meeting with Mr. Davenport. He decided that he would not tell his mother about it, partly because he didn't want her to know about the location of the trip for fear she would be cross with him. He decided to show her the drawing of the old house as Mr. Davenport had requested, however—he couldn't see any harm in that.

"Richard, dinner is ready! Come down."

"Coming, Mom," Richard said, quickly changing his clothes and putting some deodorant on, hoping that she wouldn't spot that he hadn't actually taken a shower. He ran downstairs, and they sat down to eat.

"So, tell me how it was."

"It was wonderful! Did you know it was my first time drawing outside the studio?"

"Really? I'm glad to hear you had fun. Where did you go?"

Unable to think of a response, Richard hurriedly changed the subject. "I'm starving! I'll tell you everything after dinner, and I'll show you the pictures I drew."

To Richard's relief, his mother seemed satisfied with that. Fifteen minutes later, they sat in the living room to continue their conversation.

"Come on, Richard!" his mother urged excitedly. "Show me what you drew today. I can't wait to see!"

Richard skipped over his drawings of the Balthazar house, but he showed her the other sketches of the hidden old house Mr. Davenport led him to. He pulled them from the stack of sketches he'd placed on his lap. "Here we are…here are some pictures that I drew of a lovely old house surrounded by beautiful fields."

"Oh, let me see!" Lauren quickly looked at each one, her face displaying an increasing level of shock with each new sketch. "I know this house! Oh my Lord…I can't believe it! It was my parents' house— it's hardly changed since I left it years ago."

"Mom? What are you saying?"

Lauren kept looking at the pictures with tears in her eyes for a few seconds before her eyes snapped up to meet Richard's, her voice getting louder with every word she spoke. "Wait! Did you go there? You promised me! Why did you go there?" she demanded.

"Go where, Mom?" Seeing how worked up she was, Richard realized that his mother was deadly serious, and that the house really must have been her parents' house.

She stayed silent and kept staring at him with astonishment.

Richard sighed. "OK, Mom. Yes, I went there. I'm sorry I didn't tell you; I thought that if I did, you would never let me go, and I'd miss an amazing experience with my classmates."

Lauren said nothing, but started to cry.

Richard retrieved a glass of water from the kitchen, handed it to his mother, and tried to comfort her. "Take this, Mom. It's OK, it was just a school trip to the area by the hill. We didn't go over the fence."

"It's *OK*? You must be kidding me! Promise me that you will never go near the House of Agony again." Lauren started and dropped the glass as if she was in shock at hearing herself speak those words.

"Mom, it was just a school trip, and I wasn't alone. There were many students, and two of my professors were there too."

"You are my only son, and I couldn't bear to lose you. Haven't you heard about what happened up The Hill?"

"It's OK, Mom. Please calm down. I see why you'd worry, but all this about a 'House of Agony' isn't true. It can't be." Not wanting to upset his mother more, Richard decided to change the subject. "Tell me the story of this house," he said, pointing to the one he drew.

Nodding, Lauren took a deep breath and began to calm down. "I used to live in it with your grandparents a long time ago. Soon after they passed away—the very same day, actually—I moved to live with my aunt on the other side of the city."

"What happened to it? Did you sell it? it looks like it's been unoccupied for a long time."

"No, I still own the house, but we can't move there again. It's dangerous being so close to…that place."

"Why haven't you told me this before? We've been living here for more than two years now, and you work two jobs to cover rent and pay my tuition. It doesn't make any sense!"

"I've wanted to protect you, and I was trying to keep my mind off it. I cannot imagine myself as a neighbor of what goes on over the hill."

Mom, it's one of the most beautiful places I have ever seen! We must move there."

"No!" Lauren said firmly. "I heard people left the houses near the hill and moved to the center of the city."

"Well, on my way back, I saw all the houses occupied again."

"We are *not* moving."

"Mom, we don't need to pay rent when we have a house! Life will be so much easier for you."

Richard had a long conversation with his mother, trying to convince her to move back to her old home. He gave his word to stay away from the Balthazar house and never to cross the fence, and she promised to at least think about it.

*   *   *

After that, things moved remarkably quickly. A week later, Lauren decided that they would move after all.

The rent is already paid up for the next three months, she reasoned to herself. *If things don't work out, we can always move back.*

CHAPTER FOUR

Memories Raised From The Past

It was 10am when Lauren and Richard reached the house. As she walked in, memories flooded her mind, but she sighed at the signs of disrepair. *Never mind a hill, I have a mountain to climb to get the place habitable.*

She wandered the house, her son close behind. "Nothing has changed. It's as though I left only yesterday. The furniture, the living room, the kitchen…everything's all still the same. The vase is even still on the fireplace."

Richard's tone was doubtful. "It's changed, Mom. Look at the dust, or all the spiders and mold."

Lauren blinked back tears and tried to ignore the obvious signs of neglect. She walked quickly to the living room, resting her hand on an old wing-backed chair in the corner. "Your grandpa sat here by the fireplace every morning to read the newspaper." She went into to a room containing a large window in the back of the house and pointed to a shed in the backyard. "He used to talk privately with your dad in there."

As she walked from room to room telling Richard stories, she fought to keep her voice level. To see her childhood home this deserted was heartbreaking. There were no echoes; it was as if the house refused to repeat her words, swallowing every one that came out of her mouth.

Frustrated, she shouted, "Mom! Dad! I'm home!"

A sudden gush of air rushed in, and echoes surrounded them, continuing down the hall long after Lauren had spoken. She gasped as she noticed the family photographs that still adorned the walls and the long wooden cabinet by the fireplace. She ran over to them excitedly.

"Look, Richard! This is a picture of my mom and dad." Lauren took one of the frames down and turned it towards her son.

"It's faded, Mom. They all are," Richard said gently. "You can barely make out their figures."

"Don't you see their faces, though? They look clear to me! Look, Richard," Lauren insisted, pulling another frame down. "Mom was smiling and handing me a Christmas gift here, see?"

She held the picture close to Richard's face, in the hope she could make him see his grandma, but he shook his head sadly. "I can't see anything."

Lauren showed him different pictures over and over, but all her attempts failed, and she realized that she was the only one who could see their faces. "Never mind, son," she said, turning away. "Let's take them down and put them in the basement, okay?" Without another word, she walked to her bedroom, leaving Richard taking the pictures of his grandparents down.

As soon as Lauren entered her old room, she stopped by a painting on the wall, staring silently at it for a moment. She covered her mouth and backed away until she hit the end of her bed, collapsing heavily onto it. After a few deep breaths, she gathered herself and rose to stand in front of the painting again, memories erupting in the once-dormant volcano of her mind. The painting showed Lauren and her husband; and in it, she sat on a golden chair, dressed in a beautiful white dress and wearing a precious necklace. She looked gorgeous.

*   *   *

Placing the last picture on the basement floor, Richard brushed the dust from his hands and went to find his mom.

As he walked around the house looking for her, he noticed one of the doors was open and approached it. Peering inside, he saw her stood still, staring at the back wall. He could only just make out her silhouette, and squinted against the bright sunlight streaming through the window. He crept behind her, not wanting to disturb her trip down memory lane, and joined her in looking at the painting. His eyes widened and he pointed at the canvas. "Who's that girl?" When no response came, he put a hand on Lauren's shoulders, and asked softly, "is this you?"

Lauren kept her face away in an attempt to hide her tears, and nodded slowly.

"That's impossible," he said after a long pause. "If it is you, Mom, you look like a very aristocratic lady."

A tear dropped from Lauren's eye as she continued looking at the figure who stood behind her in the painting. The man's face had faded away so much that this time, neither of them could see it.

"That's your dad." She traced his face slowly and stiffly as if her hand was weighed down with heavy chains. "That's your dad," she repeated, her voice cracking as she found herself on the verge of tears, still trying desperately to hide it.

Richard noticed her sadness and pain, and tried to comfort her. "I love the house, Mom. I'm happy to be here, and I think you will be happy too."

"I am happy. I'm home."

Richard smiled and hugged his mom. As he looked through the window, his eyes fell on the shed in the backyard. *That would be a fantastic art studio.*

"Come on, Richard, help me get this painting down."

As beautiful as he thought she looked, Richard did not try to persuade his mom to keep the painting in her room—seeing his dad's face without features would hurt them both. They carried the picture to the basement, putting all the frames in a big box in the closet down there and tightly locking the closet door.

"Come on, let's go upstairs. We have a lot to do," Lauren said, beckoning him as she climbed the stairs to the rest of the house.

"Mom, can I have the shed as my studio?" Richard asked eagerly as he followed his mother.

"Sure, son, but let's clean it first."

Suddenly, they heard a voice coming from the back door, followed by a scraping sound. It was as though somebody was trying to unlock it. Richard ran through the house to the kitchen, followed by his mom. When they got to the door, they found it wide open, the big lock still swinging in the door handle.

"Who's there?" Richard shouted.

He went to check the shed, which was still and surrounded by beautiful trees, betraying no sight or sound of another human being nearby.

A burst of birdsong and the scrape of hooves as deer wandered by the house made him breathe a sigh of relief, and he turned back to the house to help his mother clean the place.

CHAPTER FIVE

A Picture Of Davenport

Richard was delighted with their new home by The Hill. He enjoyed spending his time sitting by the fence and sketching Balthazar's house from a distance. Less than a mile separated him from the mystery, and Richard could not ignore his connection to the house—it was more than shapes for him to put on paper; a work of art he was within reaching distance of exploring.

One morning, Lauren waited at the breakfast table with a suggestion. "Richard, let's go and visit your grandparents. Their grave is on the other side of the house."

Richard followed behind his mom as they ventured outside. By her purposeful walk, it was clear she still remembered her way to their graves.

"There they are. Right by that big tree," she said as she came to a halt a few moments later. Richard remembered Mr. Davenport had told him that he lived near the very same tree. As they removed dust and leaves from what appeared to be two graves, he looked around furtively to see if he could see Mr. Davenport anywhere.

"Richard, look! I can see your grandpa's name now."

Richard bent his head to look at the name on the grave, and Immediately stepped back in shock as he saw the name on the gravestone—*Mr. Steven Davenport.* He decided not to tell his mother that the spirit of his grandfather had led him to the very house they now lived in.

* * *

Lauren saw Richard freeze, and thought that maybe it was because they used a different surname to his grandpa's. Fifteen minutes later, Lauren went inside, leaving a still-silent Richard by the grave.

* * *

Richard smelled the scent of flowers coming from the direction of the house. Many different flowers grew on The Hill, including some he had never seen before that bloomed by the Balthazar house. He was itching to go up there and discover the truth, but he had made a promise to his mother that he would not.

As he stood by the grave, Richard spoke aloud to his grandfather. "You wanted me to be here, didn't you? You weren't a dream or a figment of my imagination; you were a real man."

But how that could be? It is impossible, he thought. *Maybe the man I met was pretending to be my grandpa.*

"It's so hard for me to take in that you are lying under this stone."

Whoever that man was, the question is, why did he pretend to be my grandfather? If he was my grandfather, why did he want me to think he was dead? I wish I could see him again. Immediately, Richard had an idea that could resolve all his concerns. *I must ask my mother if she has a picture of my grandpa. That way, I will make sure the man I met was actually him.*

He headed inside and went to his mother's room. "Mom, can I ask you something?"

"Yes, of course."

"While I was at his grave, I asked myself what grandpa looked like, and I realized I have never seen a picture of him. Do you have one?"

"Yes," his mother smiled, "I do have a picture of him." She retrieved a small box from under her bed, unlocking it with a golden key she wore on a chain around her neck. The box was filled with many things that seemed to be as old as the box itself. Richard watched as she brought out a small notebook and removed a picture of a man with white hair and a healthy beard from inside. She handed it over to Richard. "This is him."

Richard stared at the picture, his eyes wide. "That's him? Oh, my Lord, that's impossible!"

"What in the world is happening, son? Why do you seem shocked?"

"Never mind, Mom." Richard tried to control his emotions, not wanting to have to explain them. "When was this picture taken?"

"Just a couple days before he and my mom had the car accident that killed them. I was in my 20s when they died."

"Can I keep the picture?"

She shook her head. "This is the only picture I have of him, and I don't want to lose it."

"OK, I understand. Mom, do you believe in ghosts?"

"Yes, I do. And I think there is evil in this world, too. That's why I don't want you to go over The Hill."

"Could a ghost come back as flesh and bones, do you think?" Richard asked.

"I don't know. I don't like to think about it. Tell me, how is your Ksenia? I haven't seen her for a while." It was evident that Richard's mother wanted to change the subject, and being worried about having to tell her the truth, Richard went along with it.

"She is OK—she's been on vacation for the last two weeks, but she gets home today. I can't wait to see her tomorrow after she's done with work. I guess I had better go and get my sketching assignment done now, so I can see her."

"OK son. just be careful, and be sure to keep your promise."

"Don't worry, Mom. You can trust me," Richard called as he left the room.

After he had seen the picture of his grandfather, there was no doubt that he had seen and talked with someone from the other side, but he had always thought that ghosts were merely foggy, transparent figures who appeared and disappeared freely. What he had seen was a real, physical human body; and that put him in a real dilemma. The man was real; he had touched him and watched him carry the large sign that was still hanging on the tree. Richard stared up at the sign then down at the earth, spotting the small hammer that the man had used was still there by the tree.

He lifted it up and said aloud, "I didn't dream this—it's solid metal."

They had walked together too, and the sound of the man's footsteps on the floor were so strong that they still resonated in Richard's mind. It was as if he was somehow experiencing two realms at the same time.

Richard went back to the grave again, holding the picture of his grandfather that he had snuck out in his hand. He shouted the man's name, but half-wondered if he should have cried "Grandpa" instead. He wished that he could see him again.

As he arrived at the graveside, he spotted a small book on the top of the gravestone. It was the same one that his grandfather had been holding in the picture. Richard picked it up with his shaking hands and gently turned its pages. They were all blank except for the first page. The ink on it was still wet, as if it had been written on moments ago. When Richard touched some of the letters, they left a black ink patch on his thumb. There were only a few words on it:

"Dear Richard,

The truth will come to you as came to me; it will reveal itself to you at certain moments."

As soon as he finished reading, the notebook turned to dust, which flew away on a sudden breeze. Now completely confused, Richard went back to the house to see if the notebook was still in his mom's box. He called her into the room and gave her his grandfather's picture.

"Mom, I thought I should return it to you. Sorry for taking it."

His mom took the picture and tried to unlock the box again, but it was already open. She searched for the notebook so that she could keep the picture between its papers once again, but it was gone. Richard now believed that there was another world trying to reach him, but his mother was distraught.

"Oh my God! I can't have lost it! The notebook was my dad's memorandum," she cried.

Lauren stopped suddenly at the sound of knocking on the front door. She quickly put the picture in her box and locked it again, then tried to compose herself and make things seem perfectly normal. When she opened the door, she was greeted by her best friend, Alyssa Stockton.

While his mom was busy with her friend, Richard decided to go and see Ksenia, his girlfriend. He felt that he needed to talk to her and invite her to visit his new home. Ksenia Stockton was also a student at the Nature School of Art, studying music. Richard had met her in the school's library—where she worked part-time alongside her studies— and had fallen in love with her right away.

Richard was a handsome man with a long pony-tail of brown hair and hazel eyes, and she was beautiful, with blonde hair and blue eyes. She had just turned 20, and was an independent girl who lived with her mom, Alyssa.

Her dream was to be a musician in the city concert, and she loved to play the flute, but she also liked to write short stories and poems.

Ksenia and Richard were planning to get married after graduation. Every day, Richard would go to the library to meet Ksenia as soon as she finished work, and they would sit together on their usual table beside the window to share stories about their days. Richard certainly had a story to share today…

CHAPTER SIX

Ksenia Walks Near The Hill

It was around 2pm on Friday afternoon, and Richard sat in the library, sketching and impatiently waiting for Ksenia to finish her first shift after her vacation, having managed to snatch just a few minutes with her during one of her breaks so far. Twenty minutes later, she came over as Richard was putting the final touches on a sketch.

She crept up behind him and put her hands on his shoulder. "What have you been sketching?"

"Hello, my darling! All done at last?"

"Yep! That was the longest day ever!" She picked up some of the sketches from a pile on the table in front of him.

"I've been working on them lately. What do you think?" Richard handed her the rest of his drawings. Ksenia admired them one by one, stopping when she saw a picture of Richard's new house surrounded by tall trees.

"I love all your drawings, but this picture stands out. Hold on, *all* these pictures seem to be of the same house, just from different angles. Oh, look at this one showing the beautiful flowers planted near its windows. It's a magical house!"

Richard felt happy hearing her praise. "Do you really like the house?"

"Yes, I do very much. Was it the one you used to live in before you moved here?"

"No, my sweetheart! Let me share with you the amazing things that have happened to me over the last two weeks."

Ksenia looked at him and nodded eagerly.

"It is my mom's house; we just moved there a week ago. Sorry I didn't tell you before—I wanted to wait until I saw you in person."

"*Your mom's* house? You must be kidding me! Your mom has a beautiful house! How has that happened? I know you could hardly make ends meet even in that little apartment."

"She inherited it. I couldn't believe it myself at first, but it's the truth."

"Where is it, exactly?"

"Just by the edge of The Hill."

"I know you're kidding me now, your mom has never even let you go there!"

"I'm not! Actually, your mom is there right now. My mom called her today, told her everything, and invited her to come and see the house."

"You're really all moved in already?"

"Yes. it all happened very fast." Richard went on to tell her the whole story, omitting the part about his meeting with his grandpa.

"Are you really choosing to live near the House of Agony when your mom even hated you *talking* about The Hill? You even tried to keep your school trip secret!"

"I know, but we have a house now, and our dream to get married can come true. Are you done for today? Let's go; our moms are expecting us to join them for dinner."

*   *   *

Fifteen minutes later, they walked up to the house. Ksenia was amazed by the beauty of the landscape. "It's magical! I did not know that a place like this could exist. I never knew about the trees or the flowers of all kinds; my mom never brought me here before." Ksenia started running and waving her hand like a butterfly flying among the flowers, but stopped short when she saw the House of Agony over the hill. As she tried to catch her breath, she averted her gaze away from it. "But what about the house over the hill? Are you really comfortable becoming its neighbor?"

"I don't believe all the stories, but to put my mom's mind at rest, I told her we could move during the few days the red light shows in the winter. It's still about a half mile away from where we live anyway, about as close as all the other houses."

"But Richard, it is the House of Agony after all. I am so scared of it." Ksenia said.

"The 'House of Agony'?" Richard repeated mockingly. "I hate to call it that, or believe that is what it is! It's so beautiful, Ksenia." Richard looked towards the abandoned house and continued, "There is something about the house; I have a strange attachment to it. Somehow, I am happier to be near that mansion than I am to have my own home." Richard stopped and thought for a moment, rubbing at a charcoal smear on his fingers.

"That scares me," said Ksenia. "If your mom heard you say that, she would be furious."

"The world is filled with nonsense stories, and this is just another one of them. One day, I will find out the truth about it, you'll see."

"Well, I want you to know I will be with you while you do. I will never fail you, Richard."

Richard kissed her hand. "I know, darling. Let's get inside, I'll give you the tour."

Once inside, Ksenia and Richard fixed some pictures on the walls while Alyssa and Lauren prepared dinner. As they decorated, Richard told Ksenia that he was planning to convert the shed into a small studio for himself. Ksenia liked the idea, and offered to help him with it.

Ksenia and her mom decided to stay with Richard and Lauren for the whole weekend. In the evening, Richard went out to gather some firewood, and the four had a wonderful time sat outside together. It was a clear night; the moon was bright, and stars were littered across the sky.

Lauren shared stories about her past, and explained that the house had always meant a lot to her, revealing stories of her childhood even Richard hadn't heard before for the first time.

"I loved this house as much as you do, Richard, but I couldn't stay here after what happened to your grandparents. Sorry, son." As her eyes filled with tears, Alyssa handed Lauren a glass of water and suggested that perhaps it was time to talk about something else. They changed the subject quickly, but a somber mood hung over them all.

*   *   *

Sometime later, both Alyssa and Lauren went inside the house, and Richard stayed outside with Ksenia.

"Tell me what your father looked like."

"I don't know. My mom said that he died three months after they got married."

Ksenia covered her mouth with her hand in shock. "Oh, I am sorry to hear that! May I ask how?"

"There was a fire. My mom said that one day she went to visit her aunt on the other side of town, and when she came back, the house she and my father shared was burned to the ground. It was horrible – my mom lost everything, including my dad. That was the reason for her leaving the city."

"Oh my God! What a very tragic story! Poor Lauren, she must be a strong woman. So that's the reason why there are no pictures of your dad, then?"

"Yeah. My mom said that the fire burned everything," Richard explained.

Changing the subject, Ksenia said, "Tell me about the place that you grew up in. Was it beautiful like our city?

"Yes, it was very quiet and small too. The people there were very nice, but I didn't have many friends. My mom never let me talk to strangers; she worried about something happening to me, as she always does."

"I think it's just that she loves you so much. She is a wise woman, and I love talking to her."

"She loves you too, Ksenia. She's decided to throw a party as soon as we've finished decorating the house, and we'd both love to have you and your mom there."

"I'd like that."

Smiling, they went inside the house and headed to bed.

CHAPTER SEVEN

Spirit From The Past

On Saturday afternoon, Lauren and Richard's friends and neighbors came to congratulate them on moving into their home.

Ksenia played her flute the whole afternoon, and all the visitors had a great time enjoying the music and the food Lauren had provided for the party, but by the time it began to grow dark at four o'clock, all the visitors had returned home.

Once they had gone, Lauren worked hard to clean and organize things again. By nine o'clock, she was exhausted and decided to go to bed early, leaving Richard in the living room sketching and doing some homework.

As soon as she laid down on her bed, she felt cold, so she covered herself with a thick blanket. She closed her eyes, and was enjoying her warm bed when suddenly she heard a weak voice.

"Open your eyes."

When she did, she noticed something strange had happened. The same picture of her and her husband she had taken down and put away in the basement now hung in its original place on the wall, and her husband was staring right at her.

She closed her eyes tightly, fighting fear. "I must be dreaming," she murmured. When she opened her eyes again she did not see the painting, but the figure of her husband himself, dressed in a black suit with a blue flower in his breast pocket. Silently, he moved to stand beside her bed and pointed to the table by the corner.

Shakily, she pulled the blanket over her head and shut her eyes again. "I am dreaming, this is a dream," she repeated.

She heard a voice calling her name. Her heart ached with how much she had missed it—it was the voice of her husband.

Pulling the blanket gently away from her face, he pointed to the flower in his pocket with a smile and walked towards the table in the corner to the left of the bed. Lauren noticed he was carrying a box covered with a green cloth.

Putting it on the table, he said, *"The flute, darling…it is time. Give it to the real owner."* His speech was slow and distant.

Lauren's eyes had followed him around the room, but as soon as she heard him speak, she covered her face again. "No!" she cried. "I must be dreaming."

Desperately, she covered her ears with her hands, but she could still hear him say, "Lauren, give it to Ksenia."

The name echoed in her mind, making her blood ran cold. After taking a few seconds to gather herself, she decided to talk to him, but upon moving the blanket away, found that he was already gone. There was no sign of him or the picture on the wall. She wondered if it might have been an illusion after all.

He looked so real, though. Could it have been him? she thought.

Lauren pulled herself out of bed to ask whether Richard had seen or heard anything strange, but as she did, she glanced at the table and was shocked to see a piece of green cloth sitting atop a wooden box. Realizing she had not been dreaming, she lifted the green fabric and opened the box to see a flute sitting inside. She gasped; it was her husband's flute.

Everything must have been as true and solid as this flute! Does that mean it was really my husband's spirit that left it here?

Her eyes scanned the room, searching for him. Just then, one of the windows opened slowly, and a breeze hit her cheeks as if it was a soft hand caressing her face. She turned to see a blue flower floating in the air towards her. As she watched it, everything froze except her tears, which dripped freely from her face. The breeze caressed her face again, as if wiping them away. At this, Lauren began to feel faint, and worried about passing out, but she stayed standing as an invisible hand placed a blue flower on hers.

Lauren looked at the blue flower, breathing in its scent as questions flooded her mind and she was taken back to the past.

We talked about that flute over 20 years ago, when he was dressed exactly like he was when I saw him moments ago. Did he really give it to me then, and just visit to leave it somewhere I could find it once he knew who I should give it to? It's solid – does that mean he's not a spirit, but in body in a different world somewhere?

Another memory flashed through her mind.

"I remember now. The letter!" she exclaimed. "You gave me an envelope and told me to keep it sealed until you asked me to open it."

At her words, the flower turned to dust that was picked up on a sudden breeze and flew out of the window.

She ran to her bed to pull her memory box out from underneath it, then turned it out on her bed, looking desperately for the letter. Her husband's handwriting stood out from the other contents, but a sudden jolt of nervousness threatened to overtake her eagerness to read it.

Suddenly the envelope flew in the air, as if someone were lifting it to hand it to her. Lauren stretched out a shaking hand to take it, feeling the spirit of her husband still with her. When she opened it, she saw a few sentences on the yellowed paper:

"My dear Lauren,

Two worlds exist, each with their own objects and people, and their own events, but what exists in one world usually cannot occupy the other. The flute was given to you years ago, but appeared for you when the time was right. However, the spirit is not so restricted. It can exist in the space between worlds, where unique and awesome things are possible."

As soon as she had finished reading, the letter turned to dust. It arranged itself to form her husband's name on the wall in front of her and then disappeared.

Lauren thought about the letter. Did that mean her husband had the ability to cross between worlds, and that she had not seen a ghost, but his living spirit? Had he known he would have to write her that letter all those years ago? No matter what the truth was, she knew she had not dreamt his apparition. She had a mission, and she knew what must be done.

She hid the flute, repacked her box, and then sat on her bed, thinking. Deciding to keep the encounter with her husband a secret from her son, she called for him.

*   *   *

"Yes, Mom? I heard you crying, what happened?" Richard said, appearing in the doorway.

"Nothing, son. It was just a dream." Her expression became graver. "Richard, I want you to tell Ksenia that I must see her."

Richard was taken aback. She had been around all day, why hadn't his mom spoken to her then? "She just left a few hours ago. Is there something that you wanted me to tell her for you?"

"No. Richard, do not come home tomorrow without her. I have something belonging to her," his mom insisted.

"OK, I'll get her from work tomorrow after my classes, and I'll try to bring her home with me."

"Thank you, that's all I need you to do. You can go to bed now; goodnight," his mom replied shakily.

Richard was worried, so rather than leave, he sat on a nearby chair. "No problem, Mom. Can I ask you what you want to give her?"

His mom shook her head, "I'm tired, leave me to have some rest. Don't forget, I must see Ksenia tomorrow."

Richard stood up and sighed, worry making his brow furrow. He had never seen his mom look so serious before. "OK, Mom. Goodnight."

CHAPTER EIGHT

The Magic Flute

The next afternoon, Richard finished his classes and went to the library to see Ksenia. She was helping a student to get a book when Richard arrived, so he sat at his usual table and waited for her to finish what she was doing.

After a couple of minutes, Ksenia walked over to him. "Hello darling, how are you?"

"Fine, but you need to come home with me now. My mom wants to see you; she said she has something belonging to you, and told me not to go home without you," Richard explained.

Ksenia shook her head. "I can't go with you today, Richard. I have to work until five."

"My mom insisted that I must have you with me when I come home. She was serious, it scared me. Please, I cannot go home without you."

"Do you know what she wanted to give me?"

"She wouldn't tell me anything other than that she has something that belongs to you, and she wants to give it to you."

Ksenia paused for a moment, then said, "Wait for me here. I will go and talk to Brianne, and ask if she can let me go early today."

Ksenia went to talk to her manager, returning soon after with a small bag in her hand.

"Everything is fine; Brianne said I could go."

"Great. What are you holding?" asked Richard.

"A gift for your mom—something she likes very much."

"So, you guys exchange gifts with each other, and there aren't any for me?" Richard joked. "Let me see it."

"No, it's a surprise!" Ksenia replied firmly.

*   *   *

When Ksenia and Richard arrived home, Lauren was waiting for them.

"Mom, we're home!" Richard shouted.

"Do you have Ksenia with you?" Lauren asked.

"Yes, Mom, I said *we* are home," Richard said with a grin as he walked into the kitchen, where Lauren was busy cooking.

She turned and smiled. "Ksenia, come and help me put the food on the table."

*   *   *

After they had enjoyed lunch together, Richard sat in the living room reading an art book while Lauren led Ksenia to her bedroom for a private talk. "Ksenia, come with me. I want to give you something."

As soon as they got into the bedroom, Lauren locked the door behind them and walked to her bedroom windows to close them. She stopped for a moment, looking at the House of Agony up the hill.

"If only I had not been so scared to be upfront with the truth," she said aloud, before falling silent again.

"What truth?" asked Ksenia.

"Nothing you need to worry about...yet."

"You had something you wanted to give me?" asked Ksenia.

Lauren walked to a small table beside her bed, picked up a long, thin box, and gave it to Ksenia. "Do you remember playing the flute for us on Saturday? Well, something extraordinary happened just after you left. I went to my bedroom, and I lay down on my bed. I was relaxing when I heard a voice, and when I opened my eyes, I saw my husband's picture on the wall, as new as if it had just been taken. In the picture, his eyes were looking at me. I was so scared that I covered my face, but when I looked at the wall again, he was there in person. He put down a box, covered by a green cloth, and left, leaving me a blue flower that made me remember something that happened 20 years ago and crumbled into dust. This is for you. Open it."

Ksenia opened the box. Inside was a unique and spectacular flute. As soon as Ksenia picked it up, a phrase suddenly appeared on its side in golden letters:

"IF THE FLUTE CHOOSES YOU, THEN PLAY ON IT. IF NOT, DO NOT TRY AND DO WHAT IS MEANT FOR SOMEBODY ELSE."

As soon as Ksenia finished reading them, all the words disappeared. The flute started glowing in her hands, and then her name appeared on it in golden letters. "This must be a magic flute!" she gasped. "I have never seen anything like this before! Did you see how the words appeared and disappeared in the blink of an eye?"

Lauren smiled. "Yes, darling. You are so special, you must be its true owner."

Overwhelmed, Ksenia gave Lauren a warm hug and kissed her cheeks. "Thank you! Thank you so much! I never thought I would have such a unique instrument. I love it, and I love you!"

"I am so happy that you like it, darling," said Lauren, settling into a chair by the window.

"I must let Richard see it!" Ksenia exclaimed, running to the door like a small child.

"Wait! Don't go, I'm not finished yet. There's something I would like you to know."

Ksenia turned to face Lauren, still examining the flute.

"Ksenia, your name is replacing my husband's. I used to see it written where yours is many years ago."

Ksenia looked up in surprise. "It was your husband's instrument?"

"Yes, it was one of the best in his collection. I heard him play it many times, and when he did, joy and happiness filled our home."

"I didn't know that your husband was a musician! Did he play music publicly?"

"No. I asked him to many times, but he used to say he wasn't allowed, because the flute was meant for someone else."

"That is so strange!" Ksenia said.

"It is. My husband had a strange relationship with his flute. In fact, before Saturday, I had never touched it before, but I saw his name appear on it many times, especially when he played music."

Ksenia nodded, listening carefully. She wanted to know everything about this magic flute.

"This present wasn't really from me, my darling. It was from my husband."

"But Richard told me that your home was burned down, and you lost all your possessions. He said that you do not even have one picture of your husband," Ksenia said, feeling both shocked and confused.

"This flute was given to me more than 20 years ago, my dear Ksenia." A couple of tears rolled down Lauren's cheeks.

"How? I'm sorry if I'm asking things I shouldn't," Ksenia said gently.

"He gave me the flute before he was gone, but I got it just yesterday. At least that's what he said."

"It took more than twenty years for the flute to get to you? Did your husband give it to someone else to pass it to you, and they took that long to do it?"

"No, my husband was the one who gave it to me yesterday." Lauren looked at a painting on the wall opposite her bed. Ksenia noticed that the picture was a painting of a man in a black suit with a cane in his hand and a woman that resembled Lauren sitting in a gold chair beside him. The painting was mostly clear, except for the man's face, which was faded and half-obscured by a shadow under the brim of the hat he wore.

"Is this his picture?"

Lauren nodded. "Yes, it was down in the basement, but I put it back up after he visited me yesterday."

"If he gave you the flute and was here, is he alive?"

"I don't know! I am more confused than you!" Lauren said. "All I know is that his name used to glow on the flute in the same way as yours does now."

Ksenia pressed her finger to the flute, rubbing the spot where her name was. "That's impossible, it looks like my name was engraved on it the day the flute was made."

"You were right earlier; It isn't a regular flute, Ksenia. There's magic in it," Lauren said. She pointed to the table beside her bed. "That's where I saw the flute last night. I always loved to listen to him; he used to play on it every morning. One unusual morning, I did not hear him playing. I asked him what on earth had happened to make him forget to play on his flute, and he said, 'I gave it away to its real owner.' He held my hand and said to me, 'Lauren, I will rely on you when the time comes to complete your mission.'

"'What do you mean?' I asked him, 'What mission you are talking about?' He smiled and said, 'Lauren, you must give the flute to her.'

"'To whom? I am not even allowed to touch it, and now you're saying I need to give something that I do not have to someone I do not know?' I exclaimed. I was as shocked and confused as you are now.

"'I just gave it to you,' he said to me. 'Lauren, I want you to remember this blue flower, then you'll know to give it to her. You'll know who when the time comes.' He pointed to a blue flower fixed on his suit.

"'Are you kidding me?' I said, 'You haven't given me anything!,' He repeated what he said about the blue flower and told me not to forget.

"'Stop trying to fool me!' I said, thinking it was a joke.

"He laughed loudly and said, 'I love you. Never mind, my darling. Forget about it for now, but keep it in mind for the future.' He looked so happy to tell me, but in time, I forgot all about the flute, how much I loved listening to its music, and everything he'd said…until he brought it to me yesterday."

"Are you saying that he did give it to you twenty years ago, but you didn't know until you saw him put it on your table last night?"

"Yes. With your name on it," Lauren added.

Ksenia worried for Lauren's sanity, and suddenly wished Richard were with them. "Lauren, let's go and show this flute to Richard. He will be so happy to see it."

"Not yet," Lauren insisted. "There's more. I know it's strange, but believe me. After a few weeks, I realized that he had truly given the flute away. When I asked him who the new owner of this flute was. He said, 'A girl. Her name is Ksenia. You won't remember her name, but the blue flower will come to you and remind you when it is time.'"

Silence fell over both of them for a moment, but then Ksenia recovered herself. Her eyes darted to the door, and she became more worried about Lauren than ever. "Let me call Richard! I believe you, but how could he have known my name even before I was born?"

Lauren didn't answer, but turned to Ksenia. "I am amazed by your music; you are such a talented girl. Your performance on Saturday still plays in my head. It was beautiful."

Ksenia realized Lauren was attempting to change the subject, but was fascinated by what she had just heard. "What was your husband's name, Lauren? I would love to know more about such a unique man."

Lauren's silence was the only response.

Is she telling the truth, or is it all to make me feel special? I must be special to her for her to give me a flute like this; it's an unbelievable, fantastic gift, Ksenia thought to herself.

CHAPTER NINE

Ksenia Plays On The Magic Flute

Ksenia remembered the gift she had brought a gift for Lauren, and broke the silence. "Come on, Lauren. Let's go to the living room; I have something for you too; I am sure you will love it."

"What is it?" asked Lauren, looking out to the beauty over the hill through her bedroom window.

In answer, Ksenia held her hand and pulled her from the chair to lead her to the living room. Once Lauren was settled in a chair, Ksenia handed her the bag she had brought with her. "Lauren, this is for you."

Inside was the second book in the *The Artist and Mermaid Eyes* series, one of Lauren's favorite stories. "Thank you, Ksenia!" she exclaimed, "The first book is one of my favorites. What a thoughtful gift. Come on, darling, we'd love to hear you play on your new flute."

Richard looked up from his art book at the mention of a new flute. Ksenia showed it to him, and after admiring it, he asked her to play. As she blew the first notes, the music was unique, but like magic, and filled the house with happiness. Still playing, Ksenia started to dance in delight. Suddenly, she noticed an extraordinary blue bird appear on one of the window ledges, where it stood watching her. It was unusual-looking; small, with a long blue tail, big strong wings, and a long beautiful neck. Its feathers seemed to be sparkling, emitting a shining light.

Ksenia stopped for a second to take a deep breath. As she paused, the bird faded, but when she blew strongly again, it became lovely and vivid once again. As she continued to play, she saw a beautiful necklace appear around his long neck, full of different sparkly blue shapes and symbols, growing bigger and bigger with the swell of the music until she could see all of its symbols. In the center, there was a sun, and its light spread brightness and beauty around everything it touched. In its heart was a blue face.

Ksenia continued playing, and watching the bird and his magic necklace. Little by little, many other shapes become visible to her under the sun's light. A sparkly star and the face of a gorgeous girl with seven flowers around her appeared for several moments, then disappeared. Ksenia's music and the sunlight swelled and dipped as one, as though they were following the same composer. As the music became softer, the necklace returned back to its normal size on the bird's neck. When Ksenia blew her last note, the bird flew to stand on a tree branch near the window.

At once, Ksenia pointed in the direction of the bird. "Look over there!" she cried.

Richard and Lauren were silent, still under the spell of the music. Ksenia cried out to them again and again, but at first, there was no response.

"What happened? Why did you stop?" they both shouted in unison as they woke up from their trances.

"The blue bird over there by the window! Look how beautiful he is," she said.

Richard and Lauren looked out of the window, but they said they couldn't see a bird.

Ksenia walked to the window until her face came right up close to the bird. He never left his place, as if he knew her. Ksenia was amazed by the beauty of both the bird and his necklace. She stared at it, and realized it looked the same as one Richard wore.

Wanting to be closer to the bird, she opened the window. Immediately, the bird flew near her face, looking at her. Ksenia stretched her hand to let the bird stand on it.

"Hello, Mom," he said.

Ksenia touched him with her other hand, the bird bending his head to rest on it as though it were a pillow. "I will come back to hear your music again, Ksenia," he said, and flew away.

Ksenia was transfixed, and in disbelief he could talk. "He was calling me 'Mom', and how did he know my name?" she murmured to herself. "Did that really happen, or did the flute send my imagination wild?"

She leaned on the window seat and kept looking at him until he disappeared into the sky. Lauren and Richard walked over to her, and Lauren put her hands on Ksenia's shoulders. "What happened, Ksenia? Why did you stop playing your beautiful music? And what are you looking at?"

"You were dancing and playing music so beautifully, darling," said Richard.

"You took me back to my past," Lauren agreed.

Ksenia turned to Lauren, gesturing to the sky. "Did you see it?"

"See what?" asked Richard kindly.

"The blue bird! He was sitting here on my hand, and he called me 'Mom'!" she gushed. "He was wearing a necklace just like the one you have."

"A bird? What are you talking about, darling? There wasn't any bird; I was watching you," Richard said.

Frustrated that neither Lauren nor Richard believed what she was saying, Ksenia went to the window and murmured, "It was here, I saw it! The blue bird touched me. He was real, and he was talking to me." She turned to Richard, "Where is your necklace?"

"Around my neck like always."

Ksenia walked over to him and looked closely at it. "It is the same as the bird's! Where did you get it?"

"I don't know. I have had it since I was a child, I guess. My mom said it belonged to my father; he passed it down to me just before he died."

"Your father? But you told me that your father died before you were born!"

"I don't know the details; Mom won't tell me." Richard glanced at his mom, then back at Ksenia. "I don't want to talk about it."

"Never mind, Richard. It's OK," Ksenia said, staring at Lauren.

CHAPTER TEN

Melody Coffee Shop

Was the blue bird real or a figment of my imagination created by the music? He was so beautiful, he really touched my heart.

Just then, Lauren interrupted Ksenia's thoughts. "Your music was fantastic, darling. You'll be famous throughout our city one day."

Richard shook his head. "You mean she'll be famous all over the world, Mom. Alyssum is the arts capital of the globe."

Both of them seemed to have ignored all that Ksenia said about the blue bird. Suddenly, she realized why she was the only one who saw it. She looked at the flute again and said under her breath, "I know why! It's because of this magic flute instrument."

"I think it's time to go public," Richard said.

"No! You know how shy I am, Richard," protested Ksenia.

"I suggest playing in the Melody Coffee Shop. I'll ask Mike to come with me and help get you a performance." Richard went on.

"Really? Why Mike?" asked Ksenia.

"His father is the director of the main theater in the city; everyone knows him," Lauren said.

"I don't think Dylan would mind if I told him about your passion for playing in his shop, but Mike will help convince him if needed," said Richard.

"That's a great idea," agreed Lauren.

"Me playing in the Melody Coffee Shop? You've got to be kidding me!"

"Why not? We believe in you, and I think people will like your music, especially with your new flute," said Richard.

Despite his encouragement, Ksenia was still worried.

Lauren patted her hand. "There's nothing to lose, darling. I don't expect there will be a lot of people there anyway. Most people stay at home around here, you know that."

"That's true," agreed Richard, "mainly because people are scared by the House of Agony." Richard looked out of the window. "We'll see the red light clearly from here," he said, bowing his head in mock fear and respect.

You make me wish we hadn't moved here, Richard. Those days will be the most horrible of my life."

"Do not be afraid, Mom. Everything will be alright. I promise you."

"I worry about you, Richard. You are all I have."

"Mom, can't you see how beautiful the house is? How could something that beautiful harm us?" argued Richard.

Ksenia still battled with her worry and cleared her throat, causing both Lauren and Richard to fall silent. "Guys, stop! I'm really nervous, and I don't even know that much about the Melody Coffee Shop."

"It is one of my favorite places ever," explained Lauren. "It might not look much, but many of the great musicians and singers started there. Who knows? It may be a good start for you."

"That's true, Mom," Richard chimed in, "Didn't your favorite pianist, Henry Alyssum, first begin to play there about 40 years ago? There was Mark Jayden, the famous violin player, and so many others as well. I think you should start playing there as soon as possible, Ksenia."

"I never in my life thought I'd play publicly in such a place, but you're right, I should go there," said Ksenia, relenting.

"I will visit Dylan tomorrow after school, and I'll take Mike along. He's heard you practice and knows how good you are, I'm sure he will be able to help."

"I promise to put my heart and soul into this," Ksenia said, pointing to the flute in her hand. "If you can help me, that would be awesome. I'll never forget it."

"Of course you won't! It'll be your first public concert!" exclaimed Lauren.

"I promise you I won't let you down," said Richard, hugging Ksenia.

*　　*　　*

The following day, Richard and his friend Mike went to the Melody Coffee Shop to meet Mr. Dylan Williams, the manager's assistant and events organizer.

The Melody Coffee Shop was on the main street in the center of Alyssum. The old building was large, built in red brick, and surrounded by marble sculptures of various musical instruments. It was widely regarded as one of the best social spots in the city, but also boasted a massive hall for new actors and artists to perform or play music in.

Open-mic parties were held every Friday and Sunday evening, and local young musicians found them an excellent place to start playing their favorite instruments in public. The place was loved by locals and visitors to the city alike, and they always enjoyed going there appreciate up-and-coming artists.

When they arrived, Richard wasted no time telling Dylan about Ksenia, her studying, and her talents, and asking him to give her the chance to play in the shop.

Dylan sighed. "As you know, we love to have new artists here. But there are procedures and rules we need to follow, especially as we've had bad experiences in the past. For us to let her play here, we need to get a request from her school. It's just too risky to have an unknown person perform without endorsement"

Richard tried to explain to him that it would not be possible to get a request from the school, because performing in a public place like the coffee shop had no connection to her studies or the school.

Dylan shrugged, and said he couldn't help until the general manager got back from vacation the next month.

Richard had been about to leave when Mike stepped in.

"Let me introduce myself, Mr. Williams. I am Mike Jones, the son of our main theater's director."

At this, Dylan's eyes widened, and his bored tone became animated. "Oh really? It's very nice to meet you. You have such a great father, Mike; he has always helped us put on great shows for our customers."

"It is nice to meet you too, sir. We respect your processes and policies, but we are looking for your help here."

"It's my pleasure to help you, Mr. Jones." Dylan looked at both men. "Has your artist played music before a public audience before?"

"No, sir, she has not, but I can assure you that she plays very well; she is a music student at the Nature School of Art," Richard replied.

"Let me see what I can do," said Dylan.

"She is an excellent musician; I wouldn't have come here today if I didn't think so. I think she is going to bring new opportunities to this place," added Mike.

"But if she's never performed publicly, that will be quite a challenge for her. What if it doesn't work out?" Dylan pondered.

"It will. I have been listening to her since last year. She always likes to play Dave Valentin music," said Mike. "I think she is such a talented girl. Will you give her a chance?"

Dylan smiled, and retrieved a large diary. "Let me check the schedule for next week. Hmm...I suggest that she comes in a week on Sunday?"

Richard hugged Mike, grinning fiercely. "Thank you. I think she will be fine; this month will be quieter, so it will be a good time for her to practice playing in front of a few people."

"Yes, business always dies down while the city waits for the red lights to appear in the House of Agony; the crowd should be smaller than usual."

"That right. Well, I will be here with my family to support her, and I will call some of my friends to come down as well," said Mike.

"I can't wait to let Ksenia know! She only has a few days to prepare, and she needs a lot of practice to be ready," Richard said excitedly.

* * *

Back at school, Ksenia was sorting books in the library when she saw Richard burst through the door breathlessly.

Worried, she ran over to him. "My darling, is everything alright?"

Catching his breath, Richard smiled at Ksenia. "Everything is great. Ksenia Stockton, you will be giving your first public performance next Sunday!"

As Richard's words registered in her mind, Ksenia's heart started to pound as a mixture of nerves and excitement filled her.

Next Sunday? There's so much to do in so few days, but how amazing! This public performance will be the start of my career as a young artist.

CHAPTER ELEVEN

Show Day

An announcement about Ksenia's performance went out in the cafe newsletter, and on the day, Ksenia's mother Alyssa, Lauren, and Richard all came to the Melody Coffee Shop to support Ksenia and listen to her play on her flute.

Ksenia herself was excited to play music in such a popular place for the first time, but also nervous as she watched the shop fill with people despite the weather being gloomy and cold.

*   *   *

For Dylan, it was unusual to see the place so packed at this time of year. He was so shocked at the crowds that he decided to call the manager of the coffee shop, Adam Stokes, to ask for his help, as he did not have enough staff on hand to serve such an unexpectedly large audience.

*   *   *

Mr. Stokes usually took his holiday at the same time every year, when no major events or big parties were organized, so he was surprised by the phone call from his assistant, asking him to come to the coffee shop as soon as he could to lead the event, as the artist performing had attracted a large. number of attendees.

"What are you talking about, Williams? It's Friday night…Wait! Are you saying she is a young artist doing an open-mic? What's her name?"

"Her name is Ksenia, and she has never played in public before," said Williams.

"Are you sure people didn't mistakenly think we were hosting an event for a famous artist? Were you responsible for the advertisement?"

"Yes, sir. I made sure to emphasize that she was a young artist making her public debut."

"Even so, why didn't you tell me before you allowed her to play?! It's dangerous to bring people out of their homes at this time of year; this event will put us in trouble with the mayor!"

"Well, to be quite honest, I didn't think I needed to. I didn't think many people would come to listen to such a new artist."

"And are there many people out there?"

"Yes! I'm surprised at how popular she is; I've never seen this happen before in all my twenty years of serving in this place, especially not at this time of the year."

"It is strange…exactly how many people are there?" asked Mr. Stokes.

"Well, there are no empty seats left. The whole place is crowded, and people are still queueing both inside and outside the building."

"Williams, are you kidding me?"

"No, sir. I'm in the office, and I can see there are still new people joining the line outside through the window. What should I do?"

"Open the larger hall for weddings and corporate events and seat them all in there. I'll be down soon."

"Okay, sir. See you then."

As soon as Mr. Stokes finished his call, he noticed a letter on his desk that had not been there a moment ago, but he recognized it at once. *"Read Me"* was written on the envelope, as well as a date and signature. The date showed the letter had been written some twenty-two years before.

"Impossible! This letter…" He put a hand to his mouth, and looked around for any sign of a person who could have planted it there. Finding none, he picked it up and examined the familiar signature. "Oh my God! It must be him."

He opened the letter:

> *"Do not be alarmed.*
> *What you see does not come from this world.*
> *Choices will not always be yours; common instinct moves*
> *people like the waves of the sea respond to the wind."*
> *It is time, the flute is going to play again. You must help*
> *Ksenia."*

"The magic flute! I can't believe it; what a special girl she is!"

It was clear now that an unseen force had compelled the crowd to be there, and would control the whole scene. Straightway, he drove to the coffee shop to help manage the event. As soon as he arrived, he parked his car and opened the car door.

As he did, a dense fog covered the whole area around the vehicle, and a man wearing a black suit emerged from the white mist. A large hood covered most of his face, but he tilted his head down as though trying to hide any identifying features that may still appear through the fog.

"You!" Stokes said, recognizing him instantly. "I just read your letter, my old friend."

The man leaned down and spoke softly as Stokes listened, nodding his head to show that he understood. As soon as the man straightened, the fog vanished, and the man disappeared with it.

Mr. Stokes called his assistant as soon as he got inside the building. "Williams, this night will be one of the best nights we have ever had. We will hear the magic music again!"

His assistant shot him a confused look. "Magic music?" he repeated doubtfully.

"Never mind, I want to see Ksenia. Come on, show me where she is."

"Yes, sir. This way, I just left her on the stage."

* * *

As Ksenia prepared to play, she heard a door open, and turned to see the assistant manager who had showed her to the stage and another man, who bowed and kissed her hand theatrically. "It is my honor to have you here, Miss Ksenia Stockton. Let me introduce myself. My name is Adam Stokes, and I am the manager of the Melody Coffee Shop."

"It is a pleasure to meet you, sir. I never dreamed I'd have the chance to play in your wonderful establishment in front of so many people!"

"I am quite sure your music will bring joy and happiness to this place and all the people in the city, even at this time of year," said Mr. Stokes.

Ksenia was happy to hear his encouraging words. "Thank you, thank you so much, sir." Her heart started beating hard, and her face turned pale as her nerves grew. "Th-thank you," she repeated shakily.

"Do not be scared or nervous. The music will flow from your heart; the flute will translate your pureness and love into beautiful music." He looked at her hand holding the flute, Ksenia saw his eyes fill with tears. He turned away and cleared his throat to keep his voice steady. "Please go and take your place. It is ten minutes to six, and there are only a few minutes left before we must start. I will introduce you to the audience myself."

* * *

Taking his place at the center of the stage, Mr. Stokes introduced Ksenia to the public as though he was presenting a very famous artist.

As soon as he got down from the stage, Mr. Stokes saw two familiar faces. Dr. Brodsky—one of the professors at the Nature School of Art, and thanks to the beliefs or Dr. Balthazar, one of its biggest challengers—stood next to the man whose face was obscured by a hood. He recognized both instantly.

"You are here, both of you!" He hugged them each in turn. "I expected to see you today, my friends. Especially you," Stokes nodded to the man with the hood.

"Come on, let's go up there," the man with the hood said, pointing towards some seats hidden away from the others. "I cannot wait to see her again."

"OK, my friend! Let's go," replied Stokes.

* * *

Ksenia stood behind the curtains of the theater, surrounded by her family and friends.

"Do not be scared, my love. You will be fine," Alyssa soothed.

"I'm so nervous. It's not going to be easy to play in front of all those people, and I feel like I've forgotten everything," Ksenia said, looking frantically through her pieces of music.

"Come on, Ksenia, don't say that! What music are you planning to play today?" asked Richard with a wide, encouraging smile.

"*The Last Leaves of Fall*, the same piece I have been practicing since last week."

"Well, if you've been rehearsing a lot, you'll definitely be fine," said Alyssa.

"But this time I am using my new flute, and I don't know if I am used to it enough yet," Ksenia whispered. Suddenly the theater organizer interrupted them.

"Are you ready, Miss Ksenia? Please take your place on the stage; we are about to start."

"Come on, darling. We believe in you," said Richard.

Ksenia left the others and went to take her place in the middle of the stage, where many microphones hung from the ceiling.

* * *

Alyssa, Lauren, and Richard took their seats at a nearby table and waited for the curtains to open. Soon, Mike and his girlfriend Megan joined them.

"It took us a while to find you guys among all these people. What on earth is going on here?" said Megan, her brows raising in surprise.

"I know, no one expected this! I hope Ksenia will do well tonight," said Richard.

Everyone was looking forward to hearing Ksenia, unaware of the force that had really brought them to hear her play.

CHAPTER TWELVE

Ksenia Plays Her Flute

The announcer welcomed Ksenia to the stage, and the theater's curtains opened. The audience burst into loud applause, and then silence dawned as they waited expectantly for her.

Taking a deep breath, Ksenia started playing on her new flute. The music she was played was unique, and it had never been heard before—it was not the piece she had practiced, but came instinctively from within her. Once she began to play, the nervousness and fear left her heart, and she watched as the notes visibly scattered and shimmered in the space around her like little stars.

* * *

For the audience, it was as if they were living in a dream, transfixed as her music waned and swelled like the waves of the sea. It carried out of the coffee shop and was heard everywhere in the city, reflecting the emotions and senses of all who heard it in a way that was different to each listener, reflecting their life experiences perfectly.

Although the music was played on one lone instrument, the audience heard an orchestra of different sounds, unique pieces echoing in every different pair of ears. Although no person heard the same thing, all felt the melodies fill their souls with happiness and light.

Ksenia herself felt like she was flying through space. The hall's walls faded, the ground melted away to reveal a landscape of snowy mountains and storm clouds. The clouds were shaped like men, and the snowy peaks had feminine shapes. As she continued to play, the clouds were replaced with a warm sun, and the stars her music formed became a necklace for each woman watching. Soon, the audience joined her in space, but they seemed not to notice. All danced happily as one.

Ksenia felt as though the flute was interpreting her feelings and the notes she played were coming straight from her heart. Suddenly, she remembered the blue bird, and wished that he was there to share her joy as she played. Sudden sadness attacked her, and her heart became empty of joy and happiness all at once. The sun and mountains disappeared, replaced by the walls and floor again. Everything darkened, reality returned as the dream world melted away, and Ksenia's feet touched the stage again.

The flute's music meant nothing to her without seeing the blue bird, and she began calling for him in sad musical notes that made the eyes of the audience red and their cheeks wet with tears. Her desire to meet the bluebird again made her look at the windows and wish that she could see him at one of them as she had before. Suddenly, she saw the bird flying towards her. She was surprised to see him—all the windows and the doors of the coffee shop had been locked carefully to avoid the cold weather outside, yet the bird was there, flying all over and circling around her. She played happy music again, delightedly dancing with the bluebird on the stage of the theater.

*   *   *

This time, Richard could see him as well. "That must be the bird Ksenia saw before—I can see him now!" he murmured in awe, standing to watch the amazing blue bird dance and sing with Ksenia. The bird was so happy that Richard was reminded of a small child playing near his mom.

I wonder where he came from? Richard thought.

He felt like the bluebird was part of him as well.

* * *

The music of the flute and the sound of the bird singing created a fantastic harmony, but no one except Ksenia and Richard could see it, so they assumed the chirps were a special note from the flute.

* * *

For Ksenia, the bird at once turned into a small boy with two beautiful blue wings. He danced with her, sometimes flying in the air around her. As Ksenia stared at him, the flute flew in the air next to her, but the music never stopped.

Ksenia moved over to the boy to hug him firmly and said, "I love you more than anything." Her eyes filled with tears as she spoke.

"I must leave now, Mom," the boy whispered in her ear before turning back into a bird.

The music stopped abruptly as happiness once again faded from Ksenia's heart. She loved the blue bird, he was her reason for playing.

"Don't go! Please stay!" she cried.

"I will come back, Mom," he replied.

The music resumed again, its sad notes reflecting Ksenia's devastation and her love for the bird. She begged him again, "Please, don't go. Stay with me."

"I can't. I have limited time here. I must leave."

Tears dropped from the bird's eye and landed on the flute, and he suddenly disappeared.

Ksenia stopped playing on her flute, and the audience were forced to leave the dream world created by her playing and return to the real world once more. They began begging her to continue, but she couldn't; she had lost her motivation. Instead, Ksenia went down the steps of the stage to join her mom and her friends. Her heart, which had been filled with happiness a second ago, had become empty again.

Her spirits were lifted as the audience clapped for her for a long time without stopping. Many of them tried to hug her and asked her for an autograph. She was happy not because the people liked her music, but because she knew that she would be asked to perform again, and when she did, the blue bird would be with her.

The night would mark a turning point in her life, she knew. She would become famous in the city, always playing music she had never practiced before. It wasn't merely a coincidence or luck, she had been chosen by a hidden world to both see and reveal true inspiration.

*   *   *

The man with a hood on his head cried loudly as Mr. Brodsky said, "You can't be here without the flute music. We must leave now."

Mr. Stokes tried to comfort him and turned to point at Ksenia. "Look down there! She is a hit, you must be so happy for her."

When he turned back to his friends, he could not find them. They had both disappeared.

CHAPTER THIRTEEN

The Blue Bird's Story

Ksenia spent the whole night after the concert thinking about the bird and admiring her new flute. The fact that she played such unique, original music on the flute only made her more curious about the secrets behind the mysterious instrument. Her eagerness to find out more made her restless, and she spent the whole night wandering in her room, deep in thought. The image of the boy with beautiful wings never left her mind.

Ksenia waited for the dawn. When the early light of the sun crept through the thick morning cloud, and the reflection of the House of Agony's red light spread through the fog, she put on a heavy coat and slipped out while her mom slept,. With no idea where to go, she looked at the flute glowing with her name. She pressed her fingers over the letters.

Who crafted my name here, and why does the blue bird show up whenever I play on it? Is the story that Lauren told me about the flute true? Can I really believe a figure appeared from nowhere to give the flute to her? If he did, why did her husband choose me to give this magic instrument to?

As Ksenia struggled to find answers to the many questions in her head, she began, almost instinctively, to walk down a long trail. The trail was framed by naked trees that lined both sides of it, the bare, dry branches rigid and brittle like skeletons. The low, dense cloud formed a shroud over her head, but offered no protection from the bleak chill outside. She looked in the direction of the house up the hill. The moment she did, the red light disappeared, settling her nerves slightly. Maybe the stranger who was visiting the abandoned house knew something she didn't, so showed her mercy? It was as though fate controlled her and the House of Agony alike.

Ksenia looked at her flute again, thinking about her blue bird and wishing that she knew everything about him, why he had come, and what he meant. Without him at her side, she was unsettled and incomplete; it was as if she was missing a piece of her heart. She wanted to play on her flute again, hoping to see him

All at once, Ksenia's thoughts pulled her under, as if she was in a dream, and she walked, entranced, down the trail to a deserted beach. A voice called to her, urging her to approach the shore. Each wave reaching the coast was like a hand stretching its fingers across the long shore to write words on the sand and then pull them into the sea, whispering them softly.

"It is time, you must know," the voice chanted again and again, its whisper almost imperceptible over the rush of the waves.

A rock shaped like a small bench emerged from the white sand of the beach near the water. *"Sit here; I am comfortable,"* it urged Ksenia.

The moment she did, the waves requested she play on her flute. *"Play, play."*

Ksenia was reluctant to obey, but she wanted to see the bird boy with blue wings again more than anything in this world, so she closed her eyes and started to play.

As she blew into the flute, music echoed across the whole coast. The cold air that had been squeezing her face turned into a warm breeze rolling in from the sea. The dream world flourished like a flower, and Ksenia opened her eyes and started to dance with her music. The waves of the sea followed.

Ksenia could make out the shape of a human being on a big wave that was making its way towards the shore. At first, sudden fog obscured the figure, but as soon as the tide reached the beach, all the fog vanished.

The wave suddenly stopped, then began spinning around as if it was dancing.

Ksenia continued playing her music, and a ray of sunlight pierced the heavy clouds to hit the wave. As her eyes adjusted to the burst of light, Ksenia saw a gorgeous girl dancing on the top of the wave. The girl was dressed in a white dress, and wore a crown cut from a single huge diamond. She looked like a princess. The wave shifted to form the figures of seven maids, who danced around her. As she stared at them, Ksenia noticed that their torsos were shaped like delicate flowers, and they were human from the waist down. Each was a different color of the rainbow, and at their appearance, the girl's dancing became even more joyful.

Just then, a bird appeared In the distance and circled the sky as though looking for someone. The flute's music started to undulate as if revealing the bird's story; filled with ventures, challenges, and a long journey, then softened.

It's expressing the bird's love! thought Ksenia instinctively.

As the music echoed, the bird pushed against the breeze. Even after he began to tire, he persisted and never gave up. Each time the wind pushed him away, he gathered himself and tried again, until eventually the wind dwindled, as if it was ashamed it had been defeated under the bird's sheer determination.

The bird flew closer until he came near the girl, his happiness and energy evident. The girl looked at him with familiar fondness, her eyes filled with affection for him. The bird drew closer and turned into a fine boy with two beautiful, unimaginably blue wings. The boy and the girl held hands and started to dance atop the wave, which rocked below them like a ship's deck. The seven maids, now carried by seven smaller waves, began to dance and sing around them in circles, sharing in their joy.

The sun's rays were interrupted by bursts of rain, the two mixing to form hundreds of tiny rainbows where the light hit the droplets. Among them, the wave drew closer to the shore. Ksenia continued playing on her flute and dancing. As she spun around, she saw all the clouds had disappeared and the sun was shining in the middle of the sky. All the trees that surrounded the beach turned green and became filled with different types of flowers of different colors—red, white, green, blue, and purple.

The breeze picked the flowers up, sending them swirling through the sky above the sea. As they floated and danced in the air, the music became very loud, its echo matching the rush of the breeze. It was as though all of creation was an instrument, played in harmony until no one sound could be distinguished from the others.

Ksenia felt like she was watching a play, and the sea was the stage of a theater. She felt as though she belonged in this fantasy world, and shared the happiness of the two lovers. Suddenly, Ksenia felt deep sorrow in her heart; and the music became slow and sad. As it did, the wave split in half, and the halves began to move away from each other. The music faded, leaving a moment of perfect silence in its wake.

As the sad music started up again, it became the boy's voice, growing louder with each silent shout that left his lips. The wave started to swallow the boy until he was fully submerged, except for a small part of his body. It was as though he was trapped by the sea, imprisoned underneath it. He waved frantically, calling out. Ksenia flew close to him, wanting to help him.

As she did, a ball of fog emerged out of nowhere. As it faded seconds later, it left a boat behind, which immediately started sailing towards the girl. The shape of a man stood on the bow of the ship, seeking the girl. She stared at him, and he stared back.

She must have promised herself to him before she met the winged boy, Ksenia thought sadly.

The girl looked between the man and the boy. Tears flooded her cheeks, falling into the sea to mix with its water. The sea's tide rose and fell as if it was breathing with sadness, but still the wave lifted the girl and placed her on the boat beside the man. The girl turned to the winged boy, and Ksenia could hear her words clearly in her head.

"You came late! You should have come before Fate made its decision."

"You should have known this was your destiny from the moment your journey started," Fate replied, whispering on the wind.

The boy thrashed around, anguished. *"Don't leave me!"* he yelled, fighting to stay afloat.

Shaking her head, the girl put her hand in the man's, and the boat sailed away.

The boy watched her go longingly. Ksenia knew his heart was broken, and she felt his loneliness. The boy called for the girl again, but she was too far away to hear. The music of the flute became sadder, and the boy's words filled Ksenia's mind; *"Let me be like a spirit watching over you. I can't live without you; I will forever be the bird watching you from a distance that landed on your ship's sail."*

CHAPTER FOURTEEN

The Boy's Destiny

As both the winged boy and Ksenia watched the boat leave, the music continued, indicating the regret of the boy and girl. The sea swelled, as though straining to contain both of their emotions.

"You do not have a place in her life. Look, she is with another man. She is meant to be with him, not with you. You ought to leave now, and you must accept your destiny," the sea said.

At that moment, Ksenia felt in her heart that the sea was trying to make him give up because it wanted to steal his strength so it could pull him deep into the water. She could see the anguish on the boy's face, and knew he was torn between accepting the situation was hopeless and giving up and his determination to keep fighting for his love.

Ksenia watched as the boy ignored what the sea said to him and continued to fight against the water that held him down. As he struggled, Ksenia's mind was filled with his thoughts again. *"Wait! She is your dream, and you must never give up,"*

Fighting with renewed energy, the boy pushed himself free of the water and flew away, following her boat. *"If I could just watch her, I would be happy for eternity. She will never know, but I will follow her like a shadow. That will be enough for me,"* the boy thought, *"I will follow her ship like a bird lost at sea; its sails will be my only roosting place."*

The notes of Ksenia's music became loud and strong, mirroring the boy's determination. The angry sea showed its frustration by launching heavy waves skyward, continuing to carry the girl away from the boy. Sudden thunder mixed with the sound of the rushing sea, matching the flute in volume. As the girl sailed away, the sun disappeared, and all the flowers died, blackened, and their petals were scattered everywhere. A sudden cold gust stripped the trees of their green, lush leaves, and the world became dark and miserable again. The flute played sad, resonant music as the beauty continued to fade from the world. The boy flew near her boat looking at the beautiful crown she now wore, shrouded in cloud so the girl could not see him.

He could not bear to see the most beautiful girl he had ever seen with another man; Ksenia knew it felt like his heart had been pierced with a whole quiver of arrows as he watched her head hang sadly, and the night wrapped around him him like a dark cloth as the universe continued to torture him. His tears whispered words of sympathy as they fell, soothing his broken heart.

Ksenia was horrified to see him so sad and broken, and her heart ached like it would burst out of her chest, but she never stopped playing on her flute. She watched as the boy's wings stilled and he plummeted from the sky to sink into the depths of the ocean. A few seconds later, his feathers rose to the surface.

As the music and the water's surface stilled, Ksenia screamed for help inside her mind, but was powerless and alone. She had seen two innocent lives destroyed by ruthless Fate, and though she cried, brokenhearted, her body felt numb with shock. The water was so clear that she could see the boy lying motionless on the sea bed beneath it, and she watched him as she continued to play. She was frightened that if she stopped, everything would disappear.

Is he gone forever? Will I really never see him again? As Ksenia cried, she was guided back down to the shore, her music soft and sad, building quietly once more.

The blackened petals gathered and fell in the water, their blackness swallowing the perfect blue. Waves stirred again, the water pushing left and right away from the center to leave an enormous hole precisely in the spot where the boy lay. A wave emerged from the bottom of the ocean to pick him up, carrying the boy to lay him down on the sand of the seashore.

As the water pulled away, the boy's body rolled slowly onto the sand of the beach. Ksenia could see one of his wings was broken. The wave gathered all his lost feathers, depositing them reverently on the seashore near the boy until they were strewn everywhere around him. Every part of his body was bleeding, and Ksenia was surprised to see that rather than being the usual red, his blood was blue. She left her flute and jumped toward him. The flute flew in the air, the music continued playing, and she knelt beside him, crying softly, her tears falling like rain on her cheeks.

She noticed the boy cried as she did, and that his eyes were hazel like Richard's. As she reached out to touch him, his form shifted to be that of the bird she had seen when playing her flute before. Gently, she cupped the bird in her hands and cradled him to her chest, sobbing loudly as his broken wing hung limply from his body and his blue blood stained her hand. Weakly, the bird lifted his head, staring at her face.

"Please tell me, who are you?" Ksenia asked thickly through her pain and sadness. "Why do you bleed blue?"

"When the time comes, you will know. This is just the start of the long journey you have ahead of you, Ksenia. You will share some of it with me and others…" the bluebird said weakly. "We are all part of the World of Inspiration."

"The World of Inspiration?" she repeated.

"It is the unseen world you go to every time you play your flute," the bluebird said. He then handed her one of his feathers and asked her to keep it with her.

At that moment, the music stopped, and the dream world and the bird both disappeared, taking with them all the feathers that had been scattered on the beach, except for the one Ksenia had been given. It was white, but stained with his blue blood. The feather told her that what she had seen was not a dream or a figment of her vivid imagination, but a real moment that had put her in touch with a different world; hidden from everyone except those who had been chosen to experience it.

CHAPTER FIFTEEN

Inspiration On The Beach

Ksenia found herself still sitting on the same rock that she had been on since she came to the beach, holding the flute in one of her hands.

"What I saw was not real, it was part of a world shaped by the spirit of my music. I must be living in a dream," Ksenia said to herself. Looking down, she gasped as she realized that the bird's white feather was still in her other hand.

Ksenia brought the feather up to her face. It still had blood on it, and blood somehow seemed to be coming out of it as well. As she clutched it close to her chest and cried, her tears somehow lay on the surface of the blood without mixing with it. They were like tiny crystals shimmering on it.

"Am I still living in that world, or am I dreaming?" she murmured. Ksenia stood and went to the place the boy had been lying in before he disappeared. When she saw the indent of his body on the sand, she realized that she was still in the fantasy world and had never left it.

"The music of the flute is not what brings me here like I suspected," Ksenia mused aloud. The sea was quiet and gloomy now—its vivid blue color had gone, and it had turned as gray as the clouds. She went back to sit on the same rock, staring brokenheartedly at the feather in her hand.

As she did, she began to cry loudly; the story of the bird had shocked her, and she could not believe what she had seen happen to him.

"He was so desperate for help, and he just had to watch as he lost everything," Ksenia sobbed. "My God, what should I do?"

She was answered by a twitch on her palm, and she ran back to the place where the boy's body had been, still holding the feather in her hand. His blood still ran from it, and it pooled in her cupped palm. When she reached the right spot, Ksenia opened her hand, and the feather flew onto the shore again, coming to rest on the sand where the boy had been lying. Once the feather touched the sand, a flat white rock rose from it. It was smooth, like a canvas, and the feather became like a paintbrush as it moved in strokes over the rock, using a steady stream of the boy's blood as paint. On contact with the rock, the blood magically changed colors over and over again until the painting was made up of all kinds of tones.

The painting was somewhere between realism and abstract art. The girl the winged boy had loved stood in the middle of the painting, shining. Her face was turned away from the viewer, towards the sea.

Ksenia realized the painting was from the perspective of none other than the winged boy, and knew that while the girl's heart and spirit stayed with him, her being had sailed with someone else, and her beautiful face and lovely eyes were lost to them.

Ksenia watched the feather silently move across the surface of the rock as it attempted to put the last touches on the painting by drawing a blue flower on the girl's dress. Ksenia knelt down, covering her mouth in awe as she watched the feather fly to rest on the blue flower, becoming part of the painting and a symbol of the spiritual bond between the boy and girl.

A sentence appeared on the sand in front of her, and the boy's voice echoed in Ksenia's head, *"In spite of all the torture and pain that you caused me, you forever inspired me."*

Ksenia burst into tears again, and did not stop crying until a big wave approached the seashore, signaling that it was time for her to go. Ksenia stood, but was otherwise unmoving, staring at the wave.

I'd leave the real world to stay here forever if I could, she thought.

Despite her longing, the World of Inspiration had other ideas. The white rock she had used as a bench sank into the sand, reappearing under her feet to hold her just above the shore itself. As Ksenia looked on, the painted white rock sank as well, becoming swallowed by the sand. Soon, the painting was fully covered by the sand, and the white rock retreated fully down into the beach.

Ksenia closed her eyes in mourning, wishing she never had to open them again. Suddenly she felt water cover her feet, and opened her eyes to see the water blanket the shore, pulling back in a movement as fluid as a breath. In its wake, Ksenia saw that the water had blackened the rocks it touched, as well as must of the sand on of the beach. The scene was like a graveyard emerging from the sand. The wind blew harshly, but Ksenia was in mourning for the bird rather than fearful, and fascinated by the mystery of the World of Inspiration. She sat on the rock and stretched her legs, feeling exhausted

"What I have seen is pure inspiration, and true love," she said. "A door has been opened to a new world, and I know it is real. I am not dreaming…" she murmured, shedding more tears. Perfect silence fell, the sea and the wind stilling as though in wait. Seconds later, the silence was broken by the sound of footsteps that were steady as a beating drum, their sound getting louder and louder as they drew close to Ksenia.

CHAPTER SIXTEEN

The Man On The Beach

As the steps stopped just behind her, Ksenia looked up to see a tall, thin man lift the hood on his jacket to cover his head. Between the hood and a cloud of white fog covering his face like a scarf, she couldn't make out any of his features.

They stared at each other for a while before the man spoke, "My child, don't cry."

"Who are you, sir?" Ksenia asked, getting to her feet.

"I am the person who had this flute before you were born."

Ksenia tried not to show her doubt. "This flute was yours, sir?" she said quickly, opening her eyes very wide. "I'm sorry, but that's impossible! A woman named Lauren gave it to me."

"I gave it to her," the man said simply, and both fell silent.

The hooded man looked out at the sea, and after taking a moment of silence to gather her thoughts, Ksenia spoke again, "But she told me her husband was the one who gave it to her."

The man said nothing.

Ksenia looked from the man to the flute and back again, before her eyes settled on him. "You are Lauren's husband, aren't you?"

The hooded man nodded silently.

"You're still alive! Lauren and Richard will be so happy to see you again. Lauren thought you were a spirit when you gave her the flute a couple of weeks ago."

Ignoring her words, the man looked at the flute in her hand and said, "I owned that flute for a long time, my name shone on it in the place yours now does for more than a decade."

"If you had it for so long, then why did you choose to give it to me?" Ksenia asked eagerly.

"It was meant for you. I have heard you playing on it often; I was there when you played in the Melody Coffee Shop."

"Really? I see! But why was it meant for me and not someone else?"

"I don't know, Ksenia. I am not the one who decided who would be the true owner—the unseen world determined your destiny."

"Unseen world? You mean the World of Inspiration?"

"Yes. It may confuse you right now, but soon enough you will know everything about it, just as I did. A long time ago, I decided to play on the flute after I found it and added it to my collection, thinking I was its true owner when my name appeared on it. I went to my room and took it out of its case, but on my first blow into it, I saw you with the bird. You were dressed in a blue dress that matched his coloring. Do you want to see him again, Ksenia?"

"Yes...oh, yes please!" Ksenia pleaded. "Can I really see him again? Is he still alive?"

"I will take you to see him. There is no time here, no limits or distance to restrict us."

As he spoke, Ksenia saw that the man knew the World of Inspiration well, and was very wise. "*Are* you alive, or are you a spirit wandering between the two worlds? Where did you come from?"

The man smiled. "No, I am real and fully alive. I am visiting you from the World of Inspiration itself."

"I see. You said you saw me with the bird? Did you see the same thing I have seen? He drowned in his boy form, then the waves washed him up on the sand." She scooped up some of the sand from the shore in one of her hands and stared at it.

"You must come with me. You have got to know everything."

"Come where, sir? What do you want from me?"

"Come on, Ksenia. Let's go to the World of Inspiration. You can get the answers to all your questions there, and you want to see the boy, don't you?"

"Yes, I do very much." Her voice shook with sadness. "I am willing to do anything…*anything*…to see him."

The hooded man commanded her to close her eyes, and she did.

"Open them again," he said after a few seconds.

Ksenia opened her eyes. At once, it felt as though she had been split in two. Half of her was still in the real world, standing on the same rock and holding her eyes closed tightly, and another part of her was looking at her body become slowly covered by mist.

Where am I? Is the girl who is still standing over on the white rock me, or am I the one who is out of her body, watching from a distance?

The man interrupted the questions which were forming in her mind.

"Open your eyes, Ksenia," he said, this time in the real world. She opened her eyes to see herself in the middle of a haze.

"Where I am, sir? I can't see anything," said Ksenia in the real world, her voice cracking and becoming weaker as she spoke. She waved her hands in the air, blindly reaching for the hooded man, emphasizing that she saw nothing.

The part of her in the World of Inspiration merely watched, trying to decipher where she was and which world lay beyond the haze. How had the split even been possible? Had her spirit—or at least part of it—gone into the World of Inspiration while her body stayed in the real world? She briefly wondered if she had died, but felt the pull of her body anchor her, confining her and limiting her movement, but reassuring her at the same time.

Suddenly, she felt herself move, and tore her eyes from her own body to look at the body that carried her spirit. She was surprised to see that it was the tall, thin body of the hooded man—Ksenia was using his eyes to see, his ears to listen, and his heart to live in the World of Inspiration.

"Let's go, Ksenia," the man said, talking to that part of her which had become part of him. The Ksenia in the real world stayed perfectly still, as if in wait for her other part to return.

As her spirit was carried forward by the man's body, Ksenia asked, *"Where are we going?"*

"Wait and see," the man replied. He waded through the mist until he reached a house. Everything except the path he needed to take was shrouded in darkness, making it difficult to recognize, but from the man's anticipation, Ksenia could tell it was important. The man entered the foyer and walked through it.

We can't risk encountering the servants, the man explained silently to Ksenia, his thought echoing around the head they shared. Carefully, he went down a flight of stairs to a small hidden room in the basement. His caution, fear and excitement rushed through Ksenia as he carefully opened the door of a room and then closed it behind him. Set into the wall in one of the corners of the room was a safe the size of a small closet. He pulled out a case and opened it to reveal the magic flute. He held the flute on his chest. As his pulse quickened, Ksenia saw that his name shone on the flute.

This must be a memory! she realized.

"There is no meaning to my life without you," the man said. "You are the most precious thing in all my collection."

Ksenia noticed that there was a harmony and admiration between the flute and the man, and realized that he was showing her the memory to prove just how much the flute meant to him even though he'd been forced to pass it onto her. The real-world Ksenia watched inside her mind.

"Do you understand, Ksenia, what the flute meant to me?"

"Yes, yes I do!" replied Ksenia's voice inside his head.

Privately, a burning question rose to the forefront of her mind. *If he had that much passion for and connection with the flute, why did he give it to me?*

Before she could probe him further, the man interrupted her thoughts. *"Let's go, Ksenia. It's time for you to learn more about who gave you the flute."*

*   *   *

The man and Ksenia's spirit left the house and returned to the beach, and the man turned his attention to the real-world Ksenia.

"It is meant only for certain people, and only they can play it," he continued aloud.

Ksenia stayed silent, watching as the sea water rose to cover her body's feet once again. In the real world, she looked down at her reflection, then at the white stone she had used as a bench gently spinning and floating in the middle of the ocean. The voice of the man echoed around Ksenia's real-world form as if it were at once in all directions. "I do not have much time left in your world."

Music filled her ears. Even though her flute remained in her hand, it was undeniably coming from the same instrument, though different from hers somehow.

The hooded man spoke again, "The music you are hearing now is mine. I am playing on the same flute that is resting in your hand in the other world—I made this journey just to be able to play it one last time. Come on, I have something to show you."

*   *   *

As he guided Ksenia's body and spirit forward, the man walked towards something flashing from a distance as though it was beckoning him. All the while, the sound of the flute and the noise and movement of the sea created a perfect harmony.

Eventually, the man reached a pole, and stretched out one of his hands to touch something hanging on it. It was an old lock. The part of Ksenia's spirit that was inside the man felt his recognition as he did. As soon he touched it, it became unlocked, and the sea fell silent. The flute music continued, but it was different. It harmonized with the breeze, and the scent of flowers filled the atmosphere. In the real world, the man whispered in Ksenia 's ears.

"I saw you as I played, and noticed how happy you were with the blue bird. I played the best music I ever had as I watched you two together."

"You saw me with the blue bird?" the real-world Ksenia asked, taking a seat on her white rock, which had appeared behind her."

"Yes, Ksenia. Look there, by that tree." As both Ksenia's spirit and her real-world self looked on, they watched a third version, who was fully in the World of Inspiration. This Ksenia sat by a beautiful tree talking to a young boy. The boy had two stunning blue wings, and both the real-world Ksenia and the spirit Ksenia recognized him as the same winged boy who had become her blue bird.

The boy flew around the tree to stand on a large blue branch, and the third Ksenia stood and leaned against its trunk. Soft music filled the scene, and the winged boy smiled at her.

"Do you like this music, Mom?" he asked her.

"Yes, it's magical," she replied.

"Soon, you will join with your instrument, and you will play just like it. The Tree of Inspiration said so!"

As he spoke, the Tree of Inspiration began to shake with excitement.

Sudden steps interrupted the scene. Ksenia's spirit knew at once who approached—part of her was still sharing his body.

Sure enough, the steps were those of the hooded man. He walked towards the third Ksenia playing the flute, but no sound escaped from it. Inside the man's body, he and Ksenia's spirit watched as their other selves met, with the Tree of Inspiration as their witness.

The winged boy flew down from his perch to land next to the hooded man. "Release the flute to the real owner."

The man lost control, and the flute slipped from his hands. It flew to rest in the boy's hand, and at once the man's name disappeared from it.

The boy with blue wings flew until he stood in front of the third Ksenia, and handed it to her. "Mom, this is yours now and forever."

When the third Ksenia had the flute in her hand, she connected with it instantly, and they became one, her name appearing where the man's had been. Ksenia's spirit watched on, feeling the hooded man's loss, and the real-world Ksenia gripped the real flute tightly, admiring the way her name gleamed on it.

"Play now, Ksenia," the winged boy said.

"I do not know how. I have never played such a flute before," the third Ksenia objected, but as she held it up to her lips and blew, unique music flowed forth.

Hearing his beloved instrument played by another, the past self of the hooded man fell to the ground in anguish; he could not bear to be separated from what had been his.

Ksenia's spirit was filled with opposing emotions—her third self's perfect joy, also but the heart-rending sadness of the hooded man with whom she shared a body. She knew he had lost everything.

*   *   *

As though she somehow sensed the pain of her spirit-self, the third Ksenia tried to console the broken man who knelt nearby, hanging his head with grief. As her joy and sadness battled each other, her music fluctuated between bright, happy notes, and pained, somber ones, at once full of both love and anger.

Just then, the winged boy flew up into the Tree of Inspiration to fetch a blue flower, which he gave to the man. As soon as the man saw the blue flower, the third Ksenia felt the sadness inside her dissipate, and her music became notes of pure joy, which spread everywhere. She watched as the winged boy and the Tree of Inspiration started to dance.

The man stood on his feet again. The blue flower now shone in his hand, and Ksenia's spirit could feel his joy return as he realized that Ksenia was the flute's true owner, and she would inspire the world with her music, as much as it hurt to give the flute up.

As the real-world Ksenia watched, knowing all this thanks to the connection between the different versions of herself, the man whispered in her ears. "Do you see who truly gave you the flute now?"

"Yes, I do," said Ksenia. At her words, the scene faded, and the sea, the air, and all the creatures became silent.

"That happened in the World of Inspiration. I was asked to deliver the flute to its real owner in the real world, but I wondered how I would find you when you lived in a time different from mine."

"When did that happen?"

"Although you have the flute now in the real world, you will be given its full power one day when you live by the Tree of inspiration in the other world," the man said.

* * *

The hooded man turned his attention to Ksenia's spirit, which still shared his body. *"Let's go. There is more to show you."*

He walked toward a stone with a date on it which Ksenia recognized as being the period two years before she was born. The man stood on it and looked at the sea. As he did, a shape matching his build grew from it and walked toward them, edging closer and closer until it merged with the hooded man's body. The man closed his eyes briefly as the bond happened, and Ksenia felt a sensation as though they passed through a wall of pressure.

* * *

When the pressure disappeared and the man opened his eyes again, he was sitting in his room and the flute was in his hand. His name shone on it no longer.

"How can I find her?" he murmured to himself.

Suddenly, a portrait of him that had been mounted on the wall fell down, replaced by a picture of what appeared to be a bedroom. In the picture, he saw his wife Lauren sleeping in a bed, but she looked more tired than usual, and had aged—he guessed she was in her forties. As he quickly stood and walked to the picture; he saw the flute resting on the table beside her bed.

"I know what I should do," the man said aloud. "I must give it to Lauren!"

Suddenly, the flute's music began to play, and the hooded man walked through the canvas to find himself in Lauren's bedroom.

From inside the man's body, Ksenia watched as the events Lauren had relayed to her unfolded exactly the way Lauren had explained them, seeing the hooded man's younger self place the flute on the table and disappear from Lauren's world and time.

"I know Lauren's story was true now!" she exclaimed inside the man's head.

"Let's go," the man said again. The image of Lauren's house faded away, and he headed down a path lined with trees whose branches and twigs reached out like gnarled fingers at the end of an outstretched arm. There was no light, but Ksenia could see clearly as they swayed in the atmosphere, and around them drifted many small floating bubbles of different sizes and shapes. Some of them looked new, bearing vivid colors, and others looked old and gray.

As the man continued to walk purposefully to his destination, Ksenia felt no confusion from him. She, however, was confused enough by this strange world for two of them, and felt very lonely as his body carried her. Although she was confused, however, the man's slow, steady heartbeat ensured she stayed calm.

A tree limb stretched toward them, its fingerlike twigs moving to release a gray bubble that drifted towards the man's body as though choosing him. The man had slowed his pace as soon as he had seen the tree; Ksenia noticed it was as if the two had been expecting each other.

Following the bubble back to the tree, Ksenia watched as an armlike limb wrapped gently around the man to keep him there. The music of the flute returned, matching the movement of the bubble. The man stretched out his hand, and the bubble rested on his palm, causing emotions to stir inside him. The bubble's gray color started to bleed onto the hooded man's body, spreading through his being like a drop of ink mixing with water. The man's body became part of the bubble, the bubble itself stretching to swallow him up inside it.

There was a moment of silence where all of both Ksenia's and the hooded man's thoughts and feelings froze, as if asleep, and then the bubble burst. All the man's senses came back, and Ksenia could hear him walking towards a big, unfamiliar house. In his mind echoed only one thought—that he needed to tell his wife that he did not have the flute anymore. Inside the house, by the fire, sat Lauren, aged around 20, talking with one of her maids.

The hooded man crossed the living room to stand in front of a big mirror at the entrance of the house, examining his face and hair.

Ksenia's spirit looked into the mirror, hoping to see his face, but she saw nothing. The mirror reflected everything except his face. Ksenia knew at once that it was not in Fate's plan for her to see his face now, if ever, because there was a time and place for everything, but she was still disappointed.

When Lauren saw him across the room, she jumped to hug him, and he kissed her.

"Hello, darling," he smiled.

"What kind of beautiful flower is this?" Lauren asked with astonishment, cupping the blue flower on his coat. "Did you find it here?"

"In our world? Definitely not!" he chuckled lightly, as though joking. "Never forget this flower, darling," he said to her, suddenly serious. "Inhale its scent, it will help you complete your mission." He took her hand, and they sat by the fireplace. "Listen carefully—what I am about to say will make no sense to you now, but you must remember it. I just gave you a precious gift."

"What, darling? Why on earth did you forget to play your flute today?" she asked him.

"I gave it away to its real owner. Lauren, *you* must pass the flute to her."

"To whom? I am not even allowed to touch it, and now you're saying I need to give something that I do not have to someone I do not know?"

"I just gave it to you. Lauren, I want you to remember this blue flower, then you'll know to give it to her. You'll know who when the time comes."

"Are you kidding me? You haven't given me anything!"

"Remember the flower. The flute will be on the table beside your bed."

"Stop trying to fool me!"

The man laughed. "I love you. Never mind, my darling. Forget about it for now, but keep it in mind for the future."

Lauren shifted uncomfortably in her seat. "OK, I got it. Please stop—you are scaring me."

"Come with me," he said. He went to the bedroom and gave her a small antique box, then showed her an envelope and asked her to keep it inside the box. "Promise me that you will never open it until I ask you to."

Lauren nodded sincerely and promised him.

*　　*　　*

"So what Lauren told me before was true!" the real-world Ksenia said in a weak voice. "I have seen everything now." Around her, silence fell, broken only by the sound of the waves.

The man approached the real-world Ksenia and ordered her to close and reopen her eyes. As she did, her two halves merged again, and her connection to the World of Inspiration faded. She stood on the white rock, holding the flute in her hand and feeling as though all her questions had been answered.

"What you see and hear in the other world is unique to you; no two people see the same. Your inspiration will be more advanced than most people as you are so special. You must protect it and keep it a secret— never tell anyone about what you have seen; the World of Inspiration is meant to be hidden. Ksenia, you are a special girl, and you will do so many great things. Your journey has just started." The man turned and walked towards the thick fog. "I must go now. Remember that you are one of very few exceptional people. Do not be afraid of your new world, but if you love the blue bird, you must never tell anyone anything about him."

"I will never say anything about the blue bird or the World of Inspiration. Its mystery will stay in my heart," she promised.

The man walked towards the fog, and Ksenia's eyes followed him until he was gone.

The man I met today was part of a different world; a world I am also part of. He must be right, I must be special and have great things in store.

She knew better now than ever before that she belonged to the World of Inspiration, and had become part of the mystery, adventure, and journey of the blue bird.

CHAPTER SEVENTEEN

The Red Light Appears

That day in Alyssum was a typically cold and wintry one. Snow covered the whole town, and the fog made it impossible for the citizens to recognize even their most familiar routes and landmarks.

Mike drove through the snowstorm to pick up Richard from his home and take him to the Melody Coffee Shop, eager to spend time with his friend before he migrated to a town nearby for winter to protect himself from the House of Agony's red light, as the wealthy and famous did every year.

As soon as Richard got into his carriage, Mike instructed his driver to continue on to the coffee shop.

"Your carriage is lovely! So warm and comfortable inside," Richard said, looking around in admiration.

"Isn't it? It's one of my dad's most prized and expensive possessions," Mike replied.

"So, where are we headed?" Richard asked.

'Melody Coffee Shop, as usual."

"Oh, my favorite place!" Richard smiled. "But do you think they will be open today?"

"Yes; I called, and Bo told me they are open until noon. After then, they will close until the evil leaves the city."

"Do you mean the stranger?" Richard asked

"Yes. I'd rather not mention him; let's talk about something else. I meant to congratulate you on Ksenia's success the other night—she was amazing!"

"Yes, she did great. She's so popular, I wonder why she hasn't been in the local news yet?"

"She will be; wait until the stranger leaves, and the city goes back to normal. The printing presses all close at this time of year."

Richard frowned, raising his eyebrows and giving Mike a doubtful look.

"You'll see, her performances will be in the news for weeks!" Mike grinned.

Richard turned his face to the window, looking out at the snowstorm. "Do you think they will allow her to play in the main concert with the famous artists?"

"I think so, but I can mention my dad if that will help. I'm always happy to support my friends," said Mike.

"Thank you, Mike. I don't know what I'd do without you."

"Don't mention it, Richard. You know we're like brothers."

"Yes, we are," Richard murmured, his tone sad.

"What's up? Come on, spill," Mike said, placing a hand on Richard's shoulder.

"Do you and your family have to move away this winter? I can't see how anything bad is going to happen."

"It's your first year here for winter, Richard. The coming days will be awful; I'm worried about you and Lauren," Mike replied.

"Yes, this is my first year, and I'll be so close to the house I'm bound to discover the truth. It's going to be fun."

"*Fun?* Why don't you and your mom stay in a hotel until the red light goes out? You'll be safe there."

"My mom suggested that, but I don't want to. Why do we need to spend money avoiding an evil that's all in our heads?"

"If money's a problem, I can rent you a hotel in the city center," Mike said, squeezing Richard's shoulder encouragingly.

"Definitely not, Mike. I couldn't ask you to do that."

"But you just said we're brothers!" Mike exclaimed.

"We are, but I don't believe the rumors. I think the threat of the stranger is merely a story made up by the Nature School of Art. They hated Balthazar's ideas, so they made the house that symbolized them and made them possible seem evil."

"But Richard, somebody always disappears at this time of year, and it's usually an artist," Mike pointed out.

Shaking his head, Richard turned to the window again to watch their approach to the coffee shop.

*   *   *

Inside the coffee shop itself, Bo prepared for their usual winter closure. The crowds that had filled the place to watch Ksenia play were long gone, and it looked empty, as it always did when the arrival of the stranger loomed. Outside, the wind blew hard, scattering snow everywhere.

Bo worked the shop alone when business dwindled like this. A man in his forties with gray hair and fair skin, he was usually employed to help clean, but was asked to keep the place open and serving coffee for the few customers that didn't stay indoors all winter waiting for the red light.

Just then, Dave Johnson, a professor at the Nature School of Art known for his classical music performances at the city's main concert hall, walked in, taking a seat at his usual table beside the window.

Bo greeted him warmly and served him, before deciding to do a deep clean ahead of closing time. "OK, let me start with those windows," he muttered to himself, putting on his heavy coat and heading outside. As he removed snow from the shop's windows, a voice called to him.

"Bo?"

"*Oh, another customer I need to take care of,*" Bo thought.

"I'll be right there!" he shouted.

"No need, I'm here to see Dave Johnson. I won't be long, you can keep doing what you're doing," the voice replied.

Bo turned, but could not see anything more than a flash of a heavy coat and a long scarf as the mysterious man quickly disappeared into the shop.

*   *   *

"Who on earth is that? He seems arrogant," Dave Johnson thought to himself as he watched and listened to the exchange outside.

As soon as the door opened, the atmosphere in the coffee shop turned cold and eerie.

The man stopped next to Dave and put a heavy hand on the table. "You don't recognize me, do you?"

Dave looked up, trying to figure out who he was. The longer he looked, the stronger the stirring of fear growing in his heart was. Though he smiled calmly, he was terrified the man was the evil stranger. "With all this stuff covering you, I need a magnifying glass to recognize you!" he chuckled nervously.

The man just stared at him silently.

"Please, have a seat. What can I help you with?"

Dave's fear grew and he felt his face pale as the man remained silent, still staring, and leaned in closer.

After a few seconds, Dave gathered himself and said, "Who are you? What do you want with me?'

As he became more uneasy, he looked around for help. He called for Bo, but the other man continued working, oblivious.

Just as Dave contemplated running from the shop, the man turned and walked back towards the main door.

Dave watched as the main door opened by itself and the man stepped through it, disappearing into the snow. His curiosity won over his fear, and he crossed to the door to watch the man go, but there was no sign of him.

Returning to his table, Dave took out his handkerchief, wiping the condensation from the glass window to see if any sign of the red light was reflected on it.

Seeing none, he breathed a sigh of relief. "Thank God," he said, "whoever I met was not the stranger."

*   *   *

There was a loud neigh outside, and a carriage man brought his horses to a stop outside the shop.

As soon as Bo saw Mike and Richard, he invited them inside and offered them a drink. They left the carriage man enjoying a warm coffee, and Bo led the other two men to a table and served them tea before going outside to finish his work.

*   *   *

"Do you see the man sitting over there? His eyes are wild, and he looks white as a sheet!" Richard exclaimed quietly, glancing at the man on the other side of the coffee shop.

"Yes, I think he is the famous Dave Johnson. He is one of the best artists in the city."

"But don't you see his face? He looks as though he has suffered a nasty shock."

"I agree," Mike nodded, leaning close to Richard. "Maybe he's scared of the stranger arriving soon?"

"Let's invite him to have some tea with us, and we can ask him."

"OK, I'll see if we can join him." Mike said.

He went over to the professor and introduced himself. There was no answer for a few seconds as Mr. Johnson continued to stare out of the window, but then he looked up. "Mike, of course! I know your father; how is he?"

"Well, thank you. I'm here with my friend Richard; may we join you?"

"S-sure, it would be my pleasure," he said shakily with a weak smile.

Mike called Richard over, who brought the tea and three mugs, and they sat together.

Mr. Johnson shared the story about the man he had just met.

"I bet he is only a nobody who wanted to scare you," Richard assured him.

"What did he look like?" Michael asked.

"He was short and very fat, but a scarf covered his face. He did not leave any footsteps on the snow behind him when he left."

At Mr. Johnson's words, Michael's eyes widened, and he turned silently to Richard.

"That's nonsense! The red light hasn't appeared, so it can't be the stranger; you all claim that's the only sign of him," Richard laughed.

Mr. Johnson and Michael stayed silent.

"Come on, the man must have been an illusion! Maybe you felt lonely and imagined him?"

I agree with Richard. I think it was only your mind attempting to scare you," said Mike.

"Perhaps. I checked the glass of the window after he left, and there was no sign of the light,"

"Cheer up, don't worry!" said Richard.

"What are you young men up to?" asked Mr. Johnson.

"I am here to say good-bye to Michael before he leaves with his family while the light is on," replied Richard.

"Mr. Johnson, are you staying here this year? I know you have another house in Mattoon you usually go to," enquired Mike.

"No, I am staying here this year; my wife is too sick to travel." He paused for a moment and added, "You're right, we haven't been in the city when the stranger is here for the last ten years."

"Then it must have been an illusion created by your fear, you're worried about staying in the city!" Richard exclaimed.

*   *   *

Outside, Bo was cleaning the windows when he saw a reflection form in the glass under his rag, at first blurrily, but then coming into focus. What he thought at first might have been a smear of dirt or a shadow cast by the trees nearby quickly took on the shape of a candle burning red.

Horror-struck, he shouted for help. "Somebody help, please! God have mercy!"

*   *   *

Hearing Bo's cry, Mike and Richard ran outside, Mr. Johnson following close behind them.

"What happened, Bo?" Richard asked

Bo did not speak, but pointed to the window.

As soon as they saw the red light, Mike immediately said, "Richard, let's go. I will drop you home, I must find my parents as soon as possible."

Richard did not reply; he was frozen in front of the window like statue gazing at the reflection of the red light.

"Come on, Richard. My parents will be waiting for me. The dark days have started; the stranger is in Alyssum again."

CHAPTER EIGHTEEN

The Bird's Visit

Ksenia lay on her bed thinking about all the things that she had experienced in the last few days. She felt a strange sense of excitement for the new adventures that awaited.

She thought about the hooded man. He had been so kind to her, and known a lot about the World of Inspiration. He had also known about the bird with blue blood, whom Ksenia loved a lot.

The idea of losing the blue bird and never seeing him again was a nightmare, and thinking about it kept her awake at night.

What I saw was almost unbelievable, but so sad! I wish I knew who the boy was so I could help him, or even so I could be sure he was alive. He was so broken, and I have no idea what happened to him.

Ksenia's emotion was like a fire stirring in her heart. "The hooded man must know," she said aloud, getting to her feet and walking to the window to look out at the beach. "I must see him; I wonder if I can get there before dark? Oh, my lovely bird! I should've asked the hooded man if there was any way I could see him again."

Ksenia felt at odds at the idea of being outside. The part of her that had lived in Alyssum and grown to fear it wanted the light to turn off and never return, but after she had promised the hooded man she would never tell anyone of the World of Inspiration, he had explained that it was a vital part of her connection to the other world. Ksenia found herself willing it to come on—if it went off forever, she would no longer be able to see her bird again.

"I must ask the hooded man to show me the way to get there freely, but for now, let me play on my flute to connect with the other world and travel to the Tree of Inspiration the blue bird loved to visit." Ksenia murmured.

She went to her closet to take the flute out, and as she did, the man's voice spoke inside her mind, *You will meet the blue bird by the Tree of Inspiration, Ksenia, you are right. You do not need your flute to connect with the World of Inspiration, it will appear to you.*

Ksenia decided she would still go down to the beach and play on her flute. She dressed in her heavy winter coat and slipped the hood over her head, then decided to sneak out—her mom would never let her leave the house while the red light burned. She left her room and went downstairs, hiding her flute under her coat and treading carefully so her mom wouldn't hear her footsteps.

As she reached the front door, Alyssa appeared from the living room. "Where are you going at this time? Look, the red light will be in the window soon! Do you want me losing you?"

Ksenia was surprised to see her mom, and struggled to think of a good response. "I want to go to see...I wa nt to...I want to go for a little walk outside, that's all," Ksenia stuttered awkwardly.

"What happened, honey? Why do you look so pale and sad? is it the light and the stranger? Don't worry, everything will be alright,"

Ksenia was too preoccupied by her concern for the bird to argue. "Yes, Mom, it's what you said. Can I go now?"

She opened the door to leave, but Alyssa shouted, "Wait for me, Ksenia! I will come with you if you insist on going out at this time; let me put my coat on."

"Mom, I want to be alone."

"I must go with you. It's too dangerous to go alone, Ksenia," Alyssa ran to the door and locked it, barring Ksenia's way.

"Never mind, I'm tired anyway. I'm going to my room to sleep."

"What happened, darling? Why are you behaving like this?"

"Like what? asked Ksenia, heading upstairs.

Alyssa went after her, gripping the handrail and stopping halfway up the flight. "You look so lost, sweetheart."

Ksenia did not reply, but ran to her room and locked the door after her.

*   *   *

Worried about her daughter, Alyssa called Lauren to ask if anything had happened between Ksenia and Richard, thinking that that might be the cause of Ksenia's sudden sadness. Lauren reassured her Ksenia would be OK, and that Richard would always love her, and never do anything to damage his relationship with her.

*   *   *

Meanwhile, Ksenia laid on her bed feeling a deep sadness in her heart. She was so anxious, and still unsure if she would see the blue bird again or not. She stared at the gloom outside her window, noting that it matched the grim sadness she felt in her heart. It was as though the life had been swallowed from the world around her.

Her eyes, which used to see only the beauty of the city and the happiness of its people, now showed her the fake joy and hope deceiving those who lived in the real would The glass of the window was suddenly covered with cloud, and the wind rattled the glass of the windowpane, firing hailstones like tiny rocks all over it in eerie shapes.

Ksenia closed her eyes and covered her face to ignore the miserable scene outside, but she never stopped thinking about the blue bird. Rain pattered against the window as the hail slowed, its sound swiftly becoming louder and deeper. Curious, she moved her hands from her face.

To her surprise, Ksenia saw the rain had melted the snow on the window, and when it had cleared, the world had been swept into the middle of spring. All the buildings around her home were gone, replaced by beautiful green fields that surrounded her and a beautiful blue sky lit up by a bright sun in the heart of it. She was still in her bed looking through the window, and her flute was beside her on a small table.

She remembered what the hooded man had said, *"You do not need your flute to connect with the World of Inspiration, it will appear to you."*

Suddenly, she heard a knock on the glass of the window. As she looked through it, she saw the bluebird staring at her and trying to get her attention.

Ksenia couldn't believe what she was seeing—the bird had come even without her using her flute!

She jumped from her bed. "You are alive, you are alive!" she exclaimed. Her heart began beating very fast, and she opened the window to let the bird in. A soft breeze swept over her face, carrying with it a pleasantly sweet smell.

Ksenia held the bird tightly to her chest as their eyes filled with tears. The bird nestled in her arms like a newborn baby and fell asleep quickly, and Ksenia lowered herself to sit with her back against the wall, careful not to wake him up.

* * *

More than an hour later, the bird opened his eyes again to see Ksenia sleeping as well. He stayed in her arms peacefully, not wanting to wake her either.

Soon, Ksenia woke up and looked at him. "I was scared that I had lost you forever," she whispered.

"You don't need to worry about me, Mom," the bird said. They fell silent, staring into each other's eyes. The silence was full of the love for each other that neither of them could explain.

* * *

Eventually, Ksenia spoke again, "Why do you call me Mom? What happened to yours?"

"She's gone," the bird said, his voice quivering. "I don't know if I'll ever see her again—she's in a different world from mine."

Ksenia began to sob loudly; it was as though he was talking about how she had been separated from him. She felt strangely connected to him. The bird bent his head down to touch hers.

"Oh, you must miss her a lot! It's OK, I will be your mom," she smiled, "Hearing you call me that makes me so happy, even though I don't have a child. I can't explain the way I feel about you, but I know I love you very much." Ksenia paused for a moment, then asked "What is your name?"

Instead of answering, the bird took to the sky, "I love you too, Mom."

CHAPTER NINETEEN

Visiting The Tree Of Inspiration

"Stay with me, please don't leave again," Ksenia begged the bird.

"I am here for a reason; to show you the way to the Tree of Inspiration." the bird replied. "I will always go there to see you."

"Where is it? I will visit it every day just to see you," Ksenia said, suddenly filled with excitement.

The bluebird flew down to stand on the table beside her bed. "Lay back on your bed and look into my eyes. When I close them, you have to do the same. Don't open them again until I tell you to."

Ksenia did as the bird had said. After her eyes had been closed for a few seconds, she heard his voice.

"Ksenia, you can open your eyes."

She opened them to find that they were the bird's, and she could see her own still closed, her head resting on the pillow as though she were sleeping.

"Where am I? Have I taken control of your body?" asked Ksenia

"You and I became one, Mom," the bird said inside her mind as the hooded man had done, *"We are using the same body so I can take you to the Tree of Inspiration."*

They flew in the air and up over the clouds, heading toward The Hill.

"It is only thirty minutes until sunset; we need to hurry," the bird told Ksenia as they drew close to the House of Agony.

"Why have we come here at this time? It's too dangerous; I'd rather not see the tree and summon you when I can in my world than risk harm to you by being in this place," Ksenia said, forgetting her own desire to see the bird as often as she could.

"Don't be scared for me!" the bird laughed loudly in her mind. Ksenia could feel him there; it was as though she owned his body, and he was an unborn child she carried and communicated with.

Ksenia looked down to see a big cloud on the ground, and watched as a beautiful tree started emerging from its heart.

Though she had seen it before, Ksenia found the Tree of Inspiration even more beautiful outside the hooded man's vision. It was very unique, consisting of seven branches each carrying a color of the rainbow; red, orange, yellow, green, blue, indigo and violet. The blue branch was the largest, and its light shone in the heart.

To Ksenia's surprise, as they approached, the tree started to wave to them.

The bird flew around the tree, landing on a nearby blue bench surrounded by flowers and all kinds of fruits. Everything shimmered a unique shade of blue.

"Are we in the World of Inspiration now?" Ksenia asked.

"No, we are in the real world, but this tree only shows here when you or I are near it. The three of us are connected."

The cloud around the tree cleared, replaced by bright sunshine, but mist still shrouded the house, creating a stark contrast.

Ksenia was amazed to learn that the Tree of Inspiration was near the House of Agony, even though she couldn't see the house itself. However, she was experiencing The Hill for the first time, and she and the bird excitedly flew everywhere, enjoying its beauty and the unique creatures that surrounded a big pond near the tree.

Everything is so magical, she thought.

Taking control, the bird hovered around the tree, coming to rest on the blue branch to look at a lone red flower growing in the middle of a sea of blue ones.

"What a beautiful flower!" Ksenia tried to go closer to it, but the bird still had control, so she breathed in its scent and asked him about it instead. "Tell me everything you know about the red flower. I feel drawn to it somehow."

I feel the same way you do, Ksenia. Whenever I miss my Mom, I come to this flower. It sings to me and tells me beautiful stories; It reminds me of you, but I'd rather be with you than it.

His words made her gain the power to dominate the bird's body again, and she held his spirit close to hers, cradling him with invisible arms.

As the sun started to set, the creatures surrounding the tree started to join with the branches that matched their coloring.

"If The Hill has all this magical scenery and lovely wildlife, why are people so scared of it?" Ksenia wondered aloud.

Avoiding giving her an answer, the bird said, *"It's time to go home, Ksenia. My mission is complete."*

Ksenia did not want to leave. She started to protest, but the bird said, *"One day you will live here and I will come to visit you every day, Mom."*

Ksenia loved the thought of seeing the bird every day, and her love for him grew as she thought about it, but she was doubtful. "Me, live here? Impossible! I could never be so close to the House of Agony." She turned her head toward it, shuddering as she saw the hand-like wisps of mist wrapped tightly around the house as though restraining a monstrous creature. "Even if it becomes the safest place on earth, Richard and I would never be able to afford to live in such an expensive house."

"You will sit here and tell me stories," the bird insisted, hovering in the air before landing on a small rock near the tree.

Ksenia wondered privately whether the bird intended her to live in another house of her own. *Perhaps he means we are going to build a cottage near the tree?*

"I will miss you every second that I am away from you," the bird said sadly.

"I will come here every day. I want to see you as often as I can," Ksenia replied passionately.

The bird took to the sky, taking her on a journey over the flowers on The Hill until it started to grow dark.

"Mom, I love you, but listen to me carefully. I will be gone for some time, but if you want to see me again, you must not go near the House of Agony to look for me. I will see you again in time, do not worry."

"But you said I would live there!" Ksenia exclaimed, confused.

"One day, but not now. I promise I will come to see you every day to see you when the time is right."

The bluebird's eyes filled with tears, showing their shared feelings. Both knew they would be apart from each other for a while.

"Let's go back," the bird said. He flew away from the tree towards her mom's house.

Ksenia turned his head to the tree to have a last look at it, wishing that she would be with her bird the next time she did.

He flew fast, racing the falling darkness, and before long, they had returned to her bedroom and her sleeping body.

Ksenia looked at her own face, which was as calm as if she was in a deep sleep. "Am I going to think that I was dreaming when I wake up?" she asked

The bird avoided her question once more, and said, *"I am going to close my eyes, imagine your spirit's eyes are also closed until I tell you to open them."*

Again, Ksenia followed the bird's instructions, and before long, she heard his voice, aloud this time.

"Ksenia, open your eyes. Your body is yours again."

Ksenia did as she was told, feeling refreshed as if she had just woken up from a long sleep.

She glanced at the window. It was split in half; one reflected the red candlelight of the House of Agony, and the other was obscured by snow and ice. It was closed tightly.

"Was I dreaming?" Ksenia wondered aloud. "Whether my experience with the bird was a dream or not, I wish I could be part of the World of Inspiration forever. I understand that the bird will always be alive and with me in my heart now."

Happiness rushed through her at the knowledge the bird had not gone forever, and as she felt her fingers brush against something in her palm, she knew her trip to the Tree of Inspiration had been real, the sight of it filling her with new excitement.

As she raised and opened her palm, she saw one of the bird's feathers resting in it.

Ecstatic, she began to dance around her room, singing, "He is alive and all that I want."

*   *   *

At the sound of Ksenia's voice, her mom knocked on her door. "What happened, sweetheart? Please open the door."

Ksenia opened the door and shouted, "I am happy, Mom, so happy!" Overjoyed, she hugged Alyssa. "I will wait for him until it is time, but he promised to see me again!"

Alyssa was confused by her words, but happy to see her daughter smile again. *I'm glad whatever dream sleep brought her cheered her up. She has a wonderful imagination, and has always loved being in her own little world…*

CHAPTER TWENTY

The Bird And The Tree Of Inspiration

After returning Ksenia to her body, the bird returned to the Tree of Inspiration again. He stood beside the tree, bending his head sadly to rest on it.

"What has happened to you, beautiful boy? Why do you look so sad? You saw your mom, didn't you?" the Tree of Inspiration asked him.

"Yes," he said, "I saw her."

The bird flew to the ground and turned into a beautiful boy of nine years old. He walked towards the tree until he leaned on it, sliding down its trunk heavily to sit on the white rock underneath it and sobbing the tears of an innocent child who had lost his mom.

The tree's blue branch bent down towards him, and a leaf wiped his tears away. "Boy, why do you cry?"

One of the other branches became a familiar swing the boy loved to be rocked on, but he ignored it. "I...I have been told that she won't be able to see me again for several years. I love her, and I want to stay here," he hiccupped through sobs.

"Did you appear to her as a bird or a boy?" the tree asked him.

"A bird; it was the only way I was allowed to see her this time. You do not know how good it felt when she hugged me. I want to be with her; I do not want to go back." He got up and turned away from the tree, still crying.

"Let's go back home. Your father is waiting for you."

"I don't want to go back! I want to stay here in this world. I want to live with her!" the boy cried.

"You are still too young to understand why you cannot," the tree said. "Come back here, boy. You must go home. You can't stay in this world."

"No, I want to stay with my mom!"

"But your dad is waiting for you. You should listen to me like you promised to. You know how much I love you, boy. I am your nanny, and you must obey your nanny."

"If you love me, then bring her here. Let her come with me and live with me and my dad," the boy said.

"You want to go back to your home and your toys, don't you?"

"No, I want my mom, nothing else. I have missed her so much. Why do all the kids I know have a mom, except me? I don't want to live in any world where she isn't."

The Tree of Inspiration realized that it would be difficult for a boy so young to understand why they had to leave, so she came up with a plan. "OK, I can leave you here if you want," the tree said to the boy, "but on one condition. You must shift back into a bird and remove this little bug from my leaf."

The boy looked up at the tree. "And if I do that, you will let me stay here with my mom?"

"Yes, I will."

"Where is it?"

"It is here," the Tree of Inspiration said, extending a limb toward him.

The boy believed her, so he shifted into his bird form and went to stand on the leaf of the tree that waited for him. The moment he did, the tree's leaves all wrapped around him to take him back to his world.

The boy returned to the world where he belonged, while Ksenia returned to her normal life.

IN THE NEXT BOOK...

Richard and Ksenia's journey will bring both of them to the World of Inspiration, where Richard will find the answers for many of his questions, including more about his father and the red light…

Ksenia will discover more about the World of Inspiration, and go on many adventures with Richard.

Together, they will find their destiny, including a surprise revelation about the House of Agony…

CPSIA information can be obtained
at www.ICGtesting.com
Printed in the USA
BVHW071322190619
551409BV00006B/163/P

9 781796 039153